COME ON, GET

LUCKY

Jacqueline Rohrbach

A NineStar Press Publication

www.ninestarpress.com

Come On, Get Lucky

Printed in the USA

Print ISBN: 978-1-64890-025-9

First Edition, June, 2020

Also available in eBook, ISBN: 978-1-64890-024-2

Warning: This book contains sexually explicit content, which may only be suitable for mature readers.

Grant is looking for love, but there's one big problem—himself. Due to Grant's massive size, not to mention the fact he's also a werewolf, all the eligible bachelors steer clear of him, preferring men who are a little less ginormous and a lot less monstrous. Only Lee, Grant's best friend and vampire extraordinaire, sees him as a gentle giant who longs to give awesome backrubs, cupcakes, and endless affection to his lifelong mate.

Lee is tired of the same old song and dance of dating and then breaking up. The only steady presence in his life has been Grant, a tried-and-true friend who always knows what to say and the right spot to scratch. So, when Grant finally breaks up with his flighty boyfriend, Lee sees an opportunity to let his carefully guarded heart out of its box and try for something real and lasting.

There's a problem, though: Lee has always forbidden romance between friends, an order he's drilled into Grant's head over and over again.

That means Lee might need to throw their friendship to the fire. To find passion, they'll have to become enemies. To find love, they'll have to get lucky.

There are only so many people who want a shifter romance dedicated to them, and I've run that list. So, I'll dedicate this one to my dogs because they don't know enough to be embarrassed. You're the goodest doggos, Nibbler and Mulder!

Chapter One

Grant wiped sweat from his brow. Hands trembling, he struggled to maneuver the oversized shirt button into its tiny hole. It was like being a virgin all over again. Should he lube the damn thing? Would that make it glide right in to everyone's satisfaction? Scratch those thoughts; Grant couldn't afford a sexual itch right now. If he stiffened, he might have a stress boner all night in the fancy restaurant where he'd booked a table for two. And, oh Jesus, everything was a mess. A total, awful mess.

"Knock, knock, big guy," Lee said, tapping on the wood frame of the doorway. "You almost ready?"

"Come on in. Help me out. Get this thing in there."

"Goodness, dear heart. I hope you won't have to say that tonight."

"I'm trying to *not* think about sex!"

"Boring."

As lithe and graceful as Grant was bulky and clunky, Lee glided in on a cloud of glitter and sarcasm. His slender fingers made quick work of the task, and before Grant knew it, his dress shirt was smoothed down the length of his torso and tucked neatly into his black slacks. Standing to the side, his palm supporting his chin, Lee inspected his handiwork. Grant, for his part, stood straight under his critical eye and endeavored not to dwell on the lingering tingle along his spine where Lee's fingers had touched him.

Muttering and twirling his finger, Lee said, "Turn around."

Grant rarely dressed to the nines because it made him feel like he was ten. Lee, who searched him over for any flaw, didn't help matters, especially not when he *tsked* like a disappointed mother.

"Well, do I pass inspection?" Grant asked him.

"Oh, you're delish. Real wagyu beef."

Grant dipped his head and made a show of inspecting his shoes to hide the sudden rush of heat to his face, which no doubt stained his cheeks a telltale shade of alarm-bell red. Then, to his mortification, he noticed a toe poking through a hole in one of his socks. Shit, he'd forgotten his shoes. Disaster. This night was going to be a total disaster.

Practically hyperventilating, Grant asked, "Where are my wingtips? The nice ones."

Lee tapped his chin. Casually, as though he'd organized Grant's closet himself, he kicked—literally—the polished wingtips onto the bedroom floor. "There are your big, goofy shoes. But, trust me, tonight is a big mistake. David is not *the one.* "

"Thanks! You're a lifesaver. I don't know what I'd do without you."

"Yes, I *know* you couldn't manage without me. But don't ignore my warning."

Wagging his finger in Lee's face, Grant said, "No, no. We're not playing the David-is-no-good game tonight. Tell me what wine should I order, instead."

"Are you asking me what pairs nicely with showing your flighty, dimwitted boyfriend your werewolf form?"

Exasperated, Grant said, "I'm bringing this one home for good, Lee."

Relenting with a sigh, Lee flounced around the bedroom, windmilling his arms in dramatic fashion as though getting ready to run a marathon. Was he stretching? Yes, yes he was. Lee hadn't surrendered: he was ramping up to continue the fight. Grant should have learned to not underestimate his best friend when it came to matters of the heart, which he saw as his expertise as a vampire. The undead, according to him, had their fingers on the pulse of life. Werewolves, well, they had their noses in its crotch. The long-term rivalry between their species was great. Truly.

Ever since Grant brought David home, Lee had gone on about how it was a poor fit. Things heated up between them when David farted and blamed Lee. Fangs out, Lee had said, "Vampires can't even pass gas. He's messing with the wrong Edward. I will glitter bomb his ass to hell. My sunlight sparkle will burn out his eyes." From there, matters got worse.

"You're being petty," Grant said, dabbing a bit of cologne on his neck. "Get over the whole fart thing. He was nervous. That's all."

"This is more than passing gas, dear heart. Although your little beau does disturb the oxygen balance of the room."

"You're a brat."

Lee said, "I *know*, dear heart. That doesn't change anything. David is... David is yuck. I'd eat him but it's an affront to my sensitive palate. *Blah*."

"Say 'blah' again but do it in a Transylvanian accent."

"If I do, you have to listen to my rant. You can't block me out, not even for a second."

Grant's inner survivalist debated the merits of the proposal. On one hand, the Transylvanian accent version of *blah* never failed to put a smile on his face, and he could use a bit of humor to settle his nerves before his big date. On the other, Lee's rants lasted as long as an immortal desired, which was a very long time indeed. Grant couldn't gnaw his foot off to get out of the trap should he decide to walk into it.

"Decisions, decisions," Lee said as a taunt without bite.

"You make it so hard."

"That's what all the guys say."

Grant stifled a laugh. "Go ahead with the rant. I couldn't stop you if I tried, so I may as well get something out of it."

"Okay, dear heart, I will keep it short. David is not your mate. He's a loser obsessed with the occult. You're...well, you're a trophy to him, something to talk about over tea with his friends. You think he's sugar, but he's NutraSweet. You don't know what he's made of, but it'll probably give you cancer. Stop putting him in your body and find the real thing."

"Feel better?" Grant asked, trying to keep his tone light. Although Lee's tongue was plenty sharp, he'd blunted it for Grant's sake. Plus, sniping at his friend never got Grant anywhere other than thoroughly tongue-lashed. Still, he'd be a lousy future mate if he didn't come to his sweetheart's defense. "I know you two don't get along, but he loves me."

"You don't need more heartbreak."

"I'm a great big werewolf. I'll be fine."

"You're mostly fluff."

"Tell that to my previous boyfriends."

Lee clucked his tongue. "It's not your fault they don't know the difference between a monster and someone who can do monstrous things. They were ninnies."

Grant's facial muscles clenched. He didn't want to talk about his last two boyfriends, both of whom knew he was a werewolf in advance and said they were fine with it, even excited. People had known of the existence of werewolves for years, after all. None of that mattered. As soon as he'd shown them his wolf form, their minds changed and he became a monster in their eyes. The pain of it, still fresh, seared away the confidence he'd built over the last few minutes.

Things weren't much better for Lee. He and his boyfriend broke up after Lee refused to have his fangs pulled in order to spend a mortal life together. Too bad Lee had a rule against dating friends; otherwise, Grant might have suggested they give each other a chance—two monster peas in a pod. The wistful thought, still painful after six years, roiled around in his heart.

"This is going to be different," Grant said, trying to work up his courage and take his mind off his conflicting thoughts. "David is different."

"No, he's heartache and trouble. And, truthfully, he's not worth either of those things. Also, *blah*, I vant to suck your blood. *Blah*. There, I did it. You're welcome."

Normally, Grant thanked the heavens his father hooked up with a vamp and that meeting had introduced him to Lee. Truthfully, Grant couldn't have picked a better brother, which is how he had to think of his eccentric vampire friend. Right now, however, he'd trade the meddlesome motormouth for a stack of beans—magic optional.

Chapter Two

With David's arm looped around his, Grant's sense of security returned. The warmth in David's chocolate brown eyes seduced Grant into believing he was right: tonight was different. Unlike the others, David saw past his size and into his heart. He understood Grant's wit was sharper than his teeth, his fur was as soft as his hands, and his claws were perfect for scratching hard to reach places. Tonight Grant found his mate.

David stared openmouthed at the restaurant's golden gilded ceiling and at its rows of perfectly aligned tables, all covered in immaculate white tablecloths. "This place is super fancy. *Shit,* I didn't forget our anniversary, did I?"

Grant smiled. "No, no. I just wanted the date to be special for us."

"You spoil me."

"Pampering my sweetheart is my job."

"Well, you're employed for life!"

Grant's heart swelled at the words, spoken with such innocence and sincerity.

They were exactly what he hoped to hear later this evening after he transformed. Sure, he was ginormous even by werewolf standards. More than a few of his own kind called his combined girth and height daunting. But being bigger than the rest didn't make him any meaner. Like Lee said, he was mostly fur.

"What are you thinking about? You got a smile as big as your, well, you know."

Okay, David could be a little immature—at least Lee wouldn't have told a dick joke in a restaurant that charged two hundred a plate—but, as far as faults went, it was a rather harmless one. Grant responded, "Just thinking about the future. That's all."

"That reminds me. I got my fortune told the other night. You'll never believe what the mystic said this time."

"Tell me."

While ripping off hunks of bread and shoving them into his mouth, David said, "She told me, get this, that because of a decision I make, my partner would find what he was looking for."

It took every ounce of willpower Grant possessed not to jump on the table to howl his glee. Excitement made his heart shoot like a rapid-fire gun in his chest. *Blam, blam, blam*: happiness circulated throughout his veins. Doing his best to sound cool, but unable to totally iron out the tremors in his voice, he said, "What do you think it means?"

"I don't know, but I didn't pay her to tell someone else's fortune. It should have been mine. You know? What happens to *me*?"

"Maybe your fate is tied to your partner's?"

"Maybe."

The lukewarm response stung, but Grant cautioned himself not to read too much into the blasé tone. David rarely spoke of his feelings, and the busy, cramped restaurant didn't lend itself to intimate conversation. He probably didn't want to gush so close to the other patrons, who might roll their eyes at anything too cutesy.

Grant said, "Well, whatever your future holds, I hope you're happy. I want that for you."

"Thanks!" David beamed. "I think I will be. Lots of good things are coming my way. I've saved enough good karma points for a Corvette."

"I don't think car dealerships accept karma."

"Why not? It's basically credit."

The comment might have been funny if David weren't serious. As it was, Grant filed the silly notion in his adorable-things-my-sweetheart-said folder. That's where his heart went to find comfort when it needed it—love pennies for emotional rainy days.

"You're doing it again."

"What's that?"

"The crocodile smile. People are staring. They probably think you're about to eat them."

Grant flinched at the description. He was tired of being typecast into the role of the fairy tale beast. After all, he hadn't locked anyone in a castle or refused to assist people in need. Quite the opposite. As a community police officer, he had helped the townspeople problem solve during his short-lived professional career. Then, when the police department he worked for drove him out for being too lenient with criminals, he'd found a new calling in the private sector and as a community advocate.

But David probably didn't mean any harm. Grant, sensitive after so much rejection, read too much into the words. That's what he told himself, anyway.

He told himself the exact same thing as they drove home. David, busy texting on his phone, nodded and made guttural noises at Grant's attempts at conversation. More than once, he burst out an agitated *shush* and waved his hand in front of Grant's face. Earlier, he'd indicated he'd had a busy day and needed time to detox from work problems. For David, that meant at least a few hours on social media, chatting away with his other friends who shared his frustrations.

"What's the spill today?" Grant asked.

"Oh, not much. Linda moved on to *another* man."

"Well, she's free to follow her heart, wherever it goes."

David rolled his eyes. "It goes to bed with anyone, apparently."

Grant grunted at the comment. Humans, unlike werewolves, put odd restrictions on sex. In Grant's mind, Linda's behavior didn't warrant any gossip, let alone derision. Consensual intimacy was one of life's great pleasures. "Maybe she doesn't know who she wants yet."

David rolled his eyes again and let out a drawn-out sigh before falling silent. His phone ticked and vibrated with each new text.

Lee's warnings pushed to the forefront of Grant's thoughts. It didn't take much imagination to see David texting his friends about his lusty relationship with a werewolf PI. Grant knew the social circle David ran in loved gossip of that flavor—the more salacious the better. Anything paranormal really sold.

"Okay, here we are," Grant said. "Home sweet home. Let me get the door for you."

Grant helped David, who was still busy with his phone, out of the car and into the house. The cupcakes he'd made, nothing fancy but homemade with love, went unnoticed on the counter. David breezed past them, making a beeline straight for the bedroom. He flopped down on the bed and beckoned Grant to follow by crooking his little finger. "Come on, I need a fix."

"Did you, uh, notice anything?"

David turned his head left and right. His expression brightened, "Oh, you cleaned the place. And did you bake for me?"

"I did! The Alton Brown cupcake recipe you love."

"Are you *sure* I didn't forget our anniversary?"

"No, you're fine. But I'm hoping to make a new anniversary out of tonight."

"Oh, I'm intrigued. Tell me?"

Feeling shy, and not quite sure how to put what he needed from David into words, Grant stalled his answer. What could he say? That he, a towering werewolf, needed validation that he wasn't some type of monster? When he dwelled on it too long, it sounded needy, not at all like the mate he wanted to be for David.

"Well?"

"I... I..."

"You? You?"

"I'm, uh."

"Oh my god, Grant. You need to shit or get off the toilet here."

That was not a line in the romantic back-and-forth Grant had envisioned for tonight. By now, rose petals should be fluttering down from the ceiling while they slow danced to David's favorite song. Instead, Grant chased around the right way to express himself like a pup chasing after its own tail. Screw words. Grant decided to stop spinning around in circles and take the leap of faith.

After a deep breath, Grant stripped off his clothes. He folded each garment and placed it neatly on the dresser.

"I like where this is going so far," David said. "Can you go faster? I need to get out of here soon to go clubbing with a few of the boys."

Okay, none of this was going the way it should have. But everything was still fine. Just fine. Nothing was out of control. He was in charge of the situation. And now he was a werewolf. Bam. There it was. Grant's ears twitched as a fly kept trying to land on his head. Thanks for nothing, generic sticky bug paper.

David's eyes widened and his jaw went slack. Almost on reflex, his thumb pressed on a button of his phone. Moments later, he babbled out a string of incoherent words and flung himself against the headboard. Head shaking, as though in constant denial, he sputtered, "Don't eat me, don't eat me, don't eat me!"

Grant shifted back to his human form. "I'm not going to eat you. I was trying to—"

But David didn't give him time to explain. He skedaddled right out of the bedroom, the house, and then the zipcode. There wasn't a cartoon dust trail marking his path, so there was a bright side for the whole mess.

Grant slumped down, letting random chance dictate where he fell. The springs of his bed creaked as they adjusted to accommodate the sudden burden of weight pressing on top of them. Grant did the same.

Chapter Three

Lee flipped his wrist and kicked his feet, which he dangled off to the side of the easy chair where he lounged. Chipper despite Grant's predicament, he said, "I'm like that guy you should have listened to at the start of a tragic play. Me: dire warning, wise advice, good council. You: whatevs, off to disaster I go."

"Thanks for your sympathy," Grant said. He'd put a bag of ice on his head to help with the splitting headache he'd developed ever since David ran out screaming. He wished he had a salve for annoying best friends.

Lee did not relent. "I like to picture you, tongue-tied and about to blubber out all your deep feelings and then just saying 'Screw that.' Seconds later, you transform and say, '*Ta-da*, I'm a werewolf.' Tell me, dear heart, did you do your zen wolf mantra before things got—please forgive me—hairy?"

The fact Lee broke down almost exactly what happened didn't improve Grant's mood one iota. "Yes, I tried zen wolf meditation. How long are you going to flog me?"

"Until I get bored of telling you that I told you."

"Anything I can do to speed up the process?"

"Listen to me for once. What did I say about vampires' and werewolves' sense of the romantic?"

Grant slid the ice pack off his head to glower at Lee. Lifting his lip, he showed a flash of teeth. Lee bared his fangs in return, adding a hiss or two for good measure. The two of them spent a ridiculous amount of time posturing before Grant, throat sore from growling, surrendered to Lee's resolve to be a pain in the ass.

"Fine. Guide me on my romantic journey."

"*Finally*, he comes to his senses. I say go screw anything that moves."

Grant smacked his lips together. "Let me bask in the poetry of your words."

"You give your big heart too easily. Try giving your dick instead."

"What sonnet are you quoting? Is it eighteen?"

"Stop trying to find Mr. Right, the white whale, the end of the rainbow, the chupacabra. Focus on making yourself happy. Be selfish for a bit. Try it on."

"Your inspiration must come straight out of a fairy tale."

Lee clucked his tongue at Grant's continued obstinance in the face of his generous wisdom dispensing. Being undead meant he had all the time in the underworld to annoy Grant. Grant, on the other hand, had a mortal's deadline. Smiling, his two incisors poking his bottom lip, Lee wiggled his eyebrows up and down.

"You look like a demonic, pervy beaver when you do that," Grant told him.

"Meow, kitten." Lee curled his hand into a claw and swiped. "That one scratched."

"You done yet?"

"Are you ready to get out there and have fun, meaningless sex?"

"No. Forgive me for wanting true love."

Dramatically—a word that described 99.9 percent of everything Lee did—he sighed and stretched. Through lowered lashes, he considered Grant, like someone who wanted to swat a pesky fly. He knew his friend too well to take the affected haughtiness personally. Lee concealed his eyes because he didn't want anyone to see the tenderness and worry there. Emotional squishiness was out of fashion for a prince of darkness.

"All right, at least tell me why I should go out and spread the love."

Lee's impish smile returned. He said, "One, it's a lot of fun. Two, it's when you stop looking that love finds you. Three, you're trying too hard and rushing yourself into relationships that don't work. I know everyone else in your pack found his mate, but you're only twenty-four. You have plenty of time to find your sweetheart. There, I gave you *three* good reasons."

Yeah, okay, Lee's argument made a certain amount of sense. Grant had to concede to at least a few of his points, anyway. He had been running himself ragged trying to keep up with his fellow packmates, who'd already gone through their courtships and were well on their way to married bliss, if not there already. Seeing everyone else paired and happy highlighted his loneliness.

Grant said, "You know, I'm going to give it a shot. You and me should go out on the town one of these nights."

Jumping to his feet, Lee clapped his hands. "I've got something even better! The vampires of my clan are throwing a fete. It'll be a grand free-for-all celebration, clothing optional, that lasts a week. Everyone there wants to hook up, so it'll be a perfect place for you to live life to its fullest amongst the dead. Besides, we could both use some time away from love and all its trappings."

"Won't they, uh, won't they be cross if a werewolf shows?"

"Only if he shows up with a cross."

"Oh, you're funny."

"I *know*. But, really, the whole vampire versus werewolves schtick is passé. All types are welcome, including hairys and humans. My clan is as accepting as they come."

"Hairys?"

"It means what you think, dear heart. Vampires are bitches, what can I say?"

Grant chuckled. While more time with Lee did sound fun, a party filled Grant with a sense of dread. Hobnobbing with vampires didn't bother him. He agreed with Lee: the whole notion of them being at odds seemed old hat, especially when they had so much in common. It's just he wasn't much of a party animal. Plus, he had a reputation in the community to maintain. He almost had a gentle refusal drafted when his phone buzzed in his pocket.

"Hold on. Let me get this."

"Now?" Lee asked.

"Yes, it's the station. They might need something."

"Right. Don't let me knot your straight laces."

Grant lifted his lips to show his teeth in jest. To the person who called, he said, "Porter here."

"Hey, man," Officer Bauer answered. He was one of the new recruits that graduated a few months before Grant was removed from the force. As a younger man, Bauer slipped into informalities every so often. Grant worried how long the naïve officer would last in such a ridged department that desperately needed progressive officers who didn't seek out opportunities to use their weapons. "Did you check David's social media page today by chance?"

"Negative, *Officer* Bauer."

"You might want to, man. It's kind of wild."

"Thank you for letting me know, *Officer* Bauer, but please don't use state property to make these types of personal calls."

"Sure thing, man. Just thought you'd like to know."

Frowning, Grant hit the end call button and thought about how he could kindly address Officer Bauer's lack of decorum. He didn't personally care, he actually believed the younger kids Officer Bauer interacted with might appreciate someone with candor and humor, but others on the force would and Grant had a duty to help the recruit succeed.

"Let me pick your brain again. There's this officer," Grant said. When no one answered, he turned around to find Lee bent over the keyboard, rapidly typing a web address into the search bar. "What are you doing?"

"What that nice officer suggested and looking at David's social media pages."

"Why?"

"Because." Instead of elaborating, Lee poked his slender finger against the screen, smudging the glass. When Grant didn't move, he said, "Well, get over here and take a gander."

Grumbling, Grant walked over and stood at his friend's shoulder. Trying to ignore Lee's scent, the wash of fresh rain, and how his silky chestnut hair shone in even the dim lamplight, Grant leaned forward and peered at the screen.

A lump—half mortification, half outrage—lodged in his throat. A snapshot of him in wolf form had been posted on Instagram mere hours after David had fled. The caption read: "Close encounter with a real monster."

Beneath it, David had typed an entirely fictional account of that night's events. Apparently, Grant had swiped at him and howled at the moon.

Lee *tsked* at an obviously photoshopped image of Grant. "My goodness. Your jaws were frothing. Someone needs dental work."

"This isn't funny," Grant bit out. "He's...he's... depicting my night of attempted romance as attempted murder. I tried to feed him cupcakes! Cupcakes!"

"Love is dead," Lee said. "Well, about that party..."

Grant checked himself before he truly flew into a rage. There was no sense in getting angry with Lee, who at least meant well. No, this was between him and David, but Grant needed space before reacting. Right now, he might actually snarl and howl if left in a room with his ex boyfriend.

"Yeah, okay," Grant said. "You know what? I'm going with you."

"Really?"

"Sure, why the hell not? I mean, it can't hurt my reputation any more than this did," Grant jerked his thumb in the direction of the computer screen, where his picture was posted for everyone to see. "I need time to think. To de-stress."

Lee, far more graceful now that he was getting his way, fluttered down to the easy chair like petals caught in a breeze. Equally airy, he said, "Excellent, dear heart. I've already booked you a room."

"Without asking me? That's so typical of you!"

Lee grinned. "I *know*. And the room is under the name Voldemutt, the wolf who shall not be named."

"What?"

"Like I said, vampires are bitches."

Chapter Four

By the time they turned up the winding road leading to the secluded hotel in the woods, Grant ran out of fingers and toes on which to count his regrets. He'd need a damn abacus before the night was through. Lee, his darling wonderful friend whom he loved more than anyone in the world, had turned the seven-hour trip into a karaoke marathon. On top of that, Lee drank himself into a stupor.

"It's your turn," Lee announced, yelling at the top of his lungs despite the close proximity and Grant's supernatural hearing.

"Keep it down. I'm sitting right beside you. And I need to concentrate. I'm driving." Grant pointed at the narrow road illuminated in the headlights. "Remember?"

"Sing!" Lee demanded. "Sing, sing, sing!"

"This is the radio, Lee. I don't even know what song is coming on next!"

"I don't want to see excuses. I want to hear results!"

"What?"

"Sing!"

Grant wished he could magnify the sound of gravel crunching under his tires to drown out Lee's ruckus. Ye gods, what had he gotten himself into? Taking on a rebound boyfriend was one thing. Traveling to the ends of the earth—an exaggeration Grant had earned based on Lee's vocal abilities—toward a rebound vampire orgy was quite another.

At least he didn't have any time to dwell on David's betrayal. Earlier, when they were in town, calls had poured in from both friends and lookiloos trying to eat a delicious scoop of his misery. Now, out in the middle of nowhere, there was nothing but tall trees cutting the sky into jigsaw pieces. His cell didn't get reception. He couldn't read texts. He couldn't see incoming calls. He couldn't hear the ding of a new email arriving. The trip gave him a convenient excuse to fall off the grid. And he was grateful.

"Hey, Grant. Grant?"

"What now?"

"Do vampires have to piss? Because I kind of feel like I need to piss."

"Hold it in. We're almost there."

Let that be true, Grant prayed. *And let my Lee pass out the moment I toss him on his bed.*

"Right. Holding it."

Up ahead, lights cut through the dense veil of black, illuminating the tree line but overpowering the stars: the first sign of civilization.

A rabbit hopped across the road. Grant sniffed the air, committing the creature's scent to memory. He doubted he'd find any sport of the sexual nature here. Lee's whole scheme started to sound raunchy rather than cathartic. But he could chase a different type of prey.

"Eat you later. Going to love getting you in my mouth," Grant said to the delicious morsel.

Lee blinked and rolled his head in Grant's direction. His mercurial hazel eyes were watering and rimmed in red. "Have you *already* found someone to fall in love with? Jesus!"

"I was talking to a rabbit!"

Lee balked. "What's wrong with you? Bunnies are... bunnies are cute. You *shouldn't* put cute things into your mouth to *eat* them, dear heart."

"You suck *human* blood."

"You...you just suck. I shouldn't have brought you here. You're going to be killjoy dad of the forest running around making up rules and...and sucking."

"Is that the best you've got?"

Lee held his fingers in front of his face and waved them back and forth. A perplexed ridge creased his forehead as his booze-sodden mind thought up a retort. Apparently, he abandoned the quest. His hand fell back to his side. "Okay, let's go get the rabbit."

"No, not now. You need to get in bed. You're...uh..." Grant stopped himself midsentence. *Acting like a drunken fool* almost slipped, but he shoved those words back into his mouth. Surprisingly sensitive, Lee would probably take offense to such a description, and he'd recently gone through his own tough breakup, which entitled him to be a mess. As his friend, Grant was supposed to give him a safe place to work out his issues. That's what this trip was about for both of them. And here he was harping on him.

But it was too late to take it back. Fangs popping out, Lee, his voice shrill and indignant, said, "I'm a what?"

"A vampire opposed to eating cute things."

Lee's eyes narrowed as he studied Grant's face. Normally, when sober, he could detect a lie from a mile away. Grant hoped inebriation dulled that part of his brain too. After a long period of consideration, Lee said, "Rabbits are goddamn adorable with their twitching noses and big floppy ears."

Grant's stomach rumbled. He coughed to mask the noise. "Agreed."

"But I am hungry, so you're going to get me food when we check in for the night."

"What are you in the mood for? Want me to scope the pool of willing blood donors when we get there?"

"Yeah, find me someone cute." Lee thought for a moment and then thrust his hand toward Grant's face. "How many fingers am I holding up?"

"Three."

"Goddamn. Make sure he's sober because I'm not."

"Cute and sober. You got it. Anything else?"

Lee thought for a moment. "Well, you might have noticed... I'm pretty drunk."

Grant stifled a laugh. Putting on a serious face, as best as he could manage, anyway, he said, "You're as articulate and charming as ever."

"I *know*! It's just...just... I don't want any potential suitors to see me...with subpar sparkle. Know what I mean, dear heart?"

"Sure do. I'll take care of it."

"You're..." He started off pretty soft and then shouted, "the best! You're going to make a great mate to some lucky fellow."

Grant's good mood deflated. During their back-and-forth, as easy and old as loafers, he forgot the reason for coming here. Heartbreak. Two loveless monsters trying their best to forget the world didn't want or need them. It was a pity party, and Lee was his plus one.

Grant allowed himself a deep sigh while he searched for a parking spot amidst the ironic hearses vampire hipsters loved to drive. His car, a clunky old Ford, stood out in the crowd, and he wondered again if the undead would really welcome him with open arms or if they'd all arch their backs and hiss at him like Lee had done when they first met. He sort of got his answer when the vampire attending the door cocked his eyebrow and pointed at Lee. "You with him?"

"He's...he's...literally holding me up," Lee said. "And he drove me here."

"What's wrong with you? Does the wolf bite?"

Lee snort laughed. "You're safe. He's got corks on his fangs."

Repressing a grumble, Grant said, "No, I don't bite. And my friend's drunk. That's all."

"You two *together,* together?" the attendant asked.

The way he said the words back-to-back, his voice tilting upward like an incredulous eyebrow, raised Grant's hackles. Lee's clan wasn't as modern as he thought if the idea of a vampire and werewolf hooking up disgusted them so much. Perhaps the outright warfare fell out of vogue, but the old resentments still thrived.

"No," Grant seethed. "We're just friends. We're actually here to get away from romantic entanglements."

The door vamp, against his better judgment if his eye roll and deep sigh meant anything, stood aside and indicated they could go forward. Before they entered the door, he put his hand against Grant's chest and gave him a shove. "No trouble, I mean it, hairy."

"Sure thing," Grant told him, pushing down his instinct to draw fangs.

"We're nothing but trouble," Lee sniped and kicked at him. "So, watch out."

The door vamp sniffed at Lee's lack of decorum but didn't say anything else. Front desk vamp wasn't much more pleasant. He curled his lip and handed Grant a key.

"There should be two," Grant told him. "One for me and one for my friend here."

Lee held up three fingers. "Yeah, two keys."

"Nope, just one. Reserved under Voldemutt." He took a second to chuckle. "You gentlemen have a good night."

Grant dragged his friend to the elevator and then through the halls while he made remarks—some pleasant, some not—at each person or supernatural they encountered. It took Grant the entire trip to process the news. They had a room. One room. Together.

Chapter Five

The hotel's décor did not reflect its out-of-the-way, rustic forest setting. Rather, it embraced an old time gothic scene with arched stained-glass windows towering upward toward the rib vault ceilings. Inside, fireplaces lent each room a cozy yet old-world atmosphere. Dark mahogany, hand-carved wood furniture contrasted against the understated cream walls. The entire effect triggered Grant's claustrophobia, but he supposed others might describe the dim lighting and cozy nooks as intimate.

"Blood or bourbon?" the vamp bartender asked them. Behind him, the bottles of liquor cast ghostly reflections on the wall.

Lee tilted his head side to side as though his bad-boy-vampire side and his office-job-vampire side warred within him. Eventually, as usual, he decided to do the smart thing. "Blood and cheesecake for me. Also, some water for my always-on-duty friend here."

"I'll actually take a shot of whisky. Or seven," Grant said.

"Oh, look at you, dear heart. One day out of uniform and you become a lush. It's only nine."

"I took this whole week off. I'm making use of it. And I don't want to hear anything from you, Count Karaoke."

Lee used the tip of his finger to slide his shades down his nose. Eyes still bloodshot and gleaming with his devilish good humor, he said, "Do I even want to ask how I got that nickname?"

"It's self-explanatory, really. Quite the musical range you have. From really terrible sounding high notes to really terrible sounding low notes and everything terrible in between."

Grant thought about teasing him more, but Lee actually seemed somewhat sheepish about last night's behavior. He'd barely muttered an apology this morning as they'd washed and readied themselves for the day. Whenever Grant tried to engage him in conversation, specifically to ask about the single room, Lee rapidly changed the subject. It wasn't like his boisterous, speech-prone friend to shy away from details.

And Grant wanted details. Ever since breaking up with Brian, Lee strictly forbid any friends-to-lovers scenario where he gambled his heart in what he described as a no-win situation. Still, the whole scenario of one room reeked of a deliberate setup for a romantic getaway between the two of them. Grant didn't want to be the type of chump who missed obvious signs, especially when his own heart ached at the possibility, but he also didn't want to anger Lee by making false assumptions either. Better to play by the rules Lee outlined.

Interrupting Grant's thoughts, Lee said, "Let's pick a table toward the back. I don't want to deal with anyone until I'm on the other end of this headache."

"Lead the way."

They sat down in one of the plush booths next to the wall.

Under the dim light of the stained-glass lamp above them, Grant tried to read his friend's mood. Lee's shape-shifter hazel eyes—a swirl of green, blue, and brown—didn't reveal much, which added to the puzzle.

Normally. The word kept shoving its way through all the others to the front of the adverb line in Grant's mind. *Normally*, Lee would be at the center of the hubbub, causing most of it. *Normally*, his light, delicate steps wouldn't clod like thunder on the hardwood floors. *Normally*, he'd be the one drinking whiskey at nine in the morning. So, what was wrong?

"Anything you want to tell me?" Grant asked. "Are you taking your breakup harder than you indicated?"

Lee winced. "No, no. And we're here because of you and David, remember?"

"Yes, but you're—"

"I'm?"

"Morose."

Incisors poking from his gums, Lee said, "I'm a vampire. Isn't being emo my dark birthright?"

Vampires shouldn't have dimples when they claimed a propensity to brood. But Lee had always been more store-brand villainous, buying the props that went along with being undead but never fully committing to the role. The vampire clan he belonged to didn't even put up that pretense. Most of them strolled around the hotel lobby in sleek modern attire that clashed with the sixteenth century vibe of the hotel. Quite a few of them wore bold, bright colors and pastels. Grant imagined they chose the venue for the same reasons they chose to drive a hearse— the irony.

Grant kept the thought to himself, but inwardly smiled each time a vamp with a cell phone walked by. Despite the lack of reception in the area, they mashed the buttons as if preforming CPR.

"I see you having yourself a private laugh at us silly bloodsuckers."

Grant grinned at Lee's annoyed, pinched face. "What? I thought vampires longed to commune with the dark elements, not their brokers."

Lee clicked his nails on the tabletop and tried to glower, but an unwilling smile tilted the corners of his mouth. "God, I miss my phone. I thought for sure the whole off-the-grid thing wouldn't be true, and I'd be able to at least check my email."

"It's for real. No reception."

"Bet you're celebrating."

Grant simulated the motion of pulling a party popper. "Confetti everywhere."

"Yeah, aren't you precious, dear heart?" Lee scrunched his nose and pushed a fork around on his plate. The prongs screeched on the porcelain. Each wince from Grant widened the grin on Lee's face.

Grant put his hands over his ears. "You. Are. A. Brat."

"I *know*." Lee put down his makeshift torture device with a clatter. Again, there was something off about the distant, vacant expression on his face, which was normally marked by his wry humor. He was hiding something, and they told each other everything.

Again, Grant thought about the single room Lee had booked for them both. Heart palpitating, his palms sweating, Grant thought about addressing the issue, just to see if he might pry some details from his oddly taciturn friend. Lee's keen eyes probed his, cutting through all the red tape of Grant's feeble outer defenses. At least Grant always felt like Lee already knew the secrets of his heart before he spoke them. But perhaps that was only Grant's own guilt nipping at his heels.

Losing his nerve under Lee's steady assessment, Grant pointed at the untouched cheesecake. "Are you going to eat that?"

Lee pushed it in his direction. "Enjoy."

"Thanks, I will."

Perhaps bringing up the single room would do little other than cause drama, but Lee's strange behavior concerned him. Grant said, "You seem really off today. I know I went through some stuff with David recently, but I'm here for you. *Always.*"

Lee looked at the table rather than at Grant. "Thanks."

"You would tell me if you needed my help, right?"

"Of course," Lee responded. "Like you said, you've always been there for me. I know I can count on you." Suddenly, his eyes started to water. The light reflecting off his tears put the swirl of blue in his irises center stage. "You've been my rock for as long as I can remember."

"I am until you tell me to piss off," Grant said with a smile. He covered Lee's hand with his. For a moment, he marveled at the odd paradox of delicacy and strength. If he wanted to, Lee could break Grant's neck in a half a second. Instead, he let himself be held and comforted.

Gently, Lee put one of his slender fingers on the back of Grant's hand and rubbed it around in a lazy circle. The sensation sent a shiver up the length of Grant's spine. He thought about planting a kiss, nothing more than a graze of his lips, across Lee's knuckles but stopped himself, withdrawing before the impulse became too strong to control.

After a long period of silence, Lee said, "The room thing. What if I told you that wasn't an accident?"

Grant shoved another generous lump of cheesecake into his mouth to keep from blurting out his feelings. Keeping his cool, but burning inside, he asked, "What do you mean?"

"I mean...what if I purposely booked our vacation so that we shared a room? What if I told you I was nervous about this trip, and that's why I got drunk? What would you say to that?"

"I'd ask you what you're nervous about."

Lee snorted and drummed his fingers on the table. That, combined with the fierce frown pulling Lee's lips downward told Grant that dragging the truth from Lee would require a more direct approach. "Okay, want to tell me why you booked a single room?"

An embarrassed flush stained his cheeks crimson. Stammering, which was very abnormal for Lee, he said, "I... I just... I thought it would be nice for us to spend time together. As...as..."

The blood from Grant's heart sung in his veins. "As...as?"

Lee flipped his hand into the air and let it flop back on the table with a thump. "As best *friends*. Okay, now promise no more questions."

"Lee..."

"Promise!"

"Fine, yes, I promise."

Tension left Lee's body. "Let's go back to the bar. I changed my mind. I want some bourbon."

As they moved through the crowd of gathered vampires, Grant tried to figure out Lee's strange mood, all while enjoying the hypnotic sway of Lee's two perfect butt cheeks that Grant would love to grab with his two big hands. Just when he decided the situation was ridiculous—that they were being ridiculous—and this whole thing was quite obviously a romantic overture, an alternative theory presented itself. There stood Brian,

Lee's ex—with his arm draped over another vampire's shoulder. When Lee saw them, his lips pursed. He turned on his heel and practically ran.

Chapter Six

"Hey," Brian said. The young cherub-looking fellow tucked under his arm waved by twiddling his fingers. Although Brian's new vampire companion appeared nice enough, even dorky in his checkered shorts and polo shirt, Grant scowled at the duo out of loyalty to Lee. Otherwise, he'd have saved his enmity for Brian, who had a lot of gall coming here.

"Hey," Grant said back. "You guys here all week?"

"Afraid so," Brian said. "Are you and the drama queen in for the long haul?"

Was Lee prone to drama? Okay, *yes*. But it was a charming characteristic focused on using glib humor to cheer others, not the selfish brand where he bent the world to revolve around him. Lee wasn't selfish, just lavishly fabulous, and he had enough sparkle for everyone.

Grant suppressed a growl. "Unknown."

"Yes, I suppose it'll depend on Lee's mood. One second he'll be madly in love with you, the next he'll tell you his fangs mean more than anything else in the world. That and his nest of freaks—sorry, his clan."

Grant took a moment to study the reaction of Brian's new vampire beau, who still hadn't offered his name, so Grant decided to call him Cherub. Surely, Cherub wouldn't endure such open hostility toward his clan. Sweet-faced with not even a hint of facial hair on his smooth cheeks, he tilted his head to the side and said, "Oh, I agree with him. This is going to be my last run as a vampire. Brian brought me here as a little going away party. After we leave here, we're starting a new life. One where we'll both enjoy the coil of mortality."

"How sweet of him to give you that," Grant managed, though he secretly hoped the coil of mortality wrapped its nose around Brian's neck. "Well, see you two later."

"Yes, give Lee my best," Brian said, patting Cherub's hand. "Let him know I found someone who knows what love means."

"I'll be sure to *not* do that," Grant said.

As he walked back to the room, several vampires checked out his body and graced him with coy, inviting smiles. One, a bold hipster with tight jeans and a grunge band T-shirt, lifted his shirt to reveal a slender yet muscular stomach. On it, he had a tattoo that read "your mouth here." He puckered his lips and blew Grant a kiss.

Grant had come here to hook up, so why did his eyes barely rove over the offered goods, which were on the block and enticing? An easy explanation didn't come to mind. Instead of dwelling on the issue, he plowed straight ahead—pushing his way through the gathered crowd in the lobby and then all the way up the stairs. Stupidly, forgetting they were sharing a room, Grant tapped lightly on the door and waited.

Lee cracked open the door until the sliding door lock pulled taut. Lips pursed into an expression Grant associated with annoyance, he glared through the narrow slit and opened his mouth to speak. When he saw Grant, he brightened. "Oh, it's you."

"Yeah, it's me. Did you think I'd stay downstairs after you fled?"

"Sort of."

"Well, are you going to let me in?"

Lee didn't move away from the door. He drummed his fingers on the wood and made a show of considering Grant's request. There it was: the drama queen in him. But Grant didn't take it personally, not since he knew the reason for the hesitation. Lee, the caretaker in every relationship he'd ever had, hated being taken care of. He always appeared with the chicken noodle soup and a cheery smile, ready to wipe brows with cool cloths and take temperatures. Not the other way around.

"Come on," Grant said, prodding him. "I'll let you give me lengthy advice without protest."

Lee shrugged. "I brought you here to party, not to hide in the room. Go back out there," Lee said, shooing him by flipping his fingers forward. "Go find yourself an easy lay and screw yourself to oblivion."

"Seriously, where do you find these lines? Do angels whisper them in your ear? That's it. I'm sure."

"From their lips, to my mouth, to your ears, dear heart. Now, seriously, go fetch while you look so fetching."

"And the wordplay. What would Dracula say if he were here?"

"*Blah*, leave Lee alone. He's grumpy. *Blah*."

"Somehow I don't think that's it."

Lee waved his hand in front of his face to get into character. "*Blah*, my cape keeps getting stuck in the door. *Blah*."

"Such are the practical limitations of high fashion."

Lee's lips quirked in an impish smile that softened his aristocratic sharp features. "But, seriously, go out there and have fun. I brought you here to forget about David, not to lock yourself in the bat cave with me."

"Come on, let me in."

"No, no. Go have fun."

"Don't make me break down the door."

Lee sighed. "You werewolves. Always so dramatic."

"Did you just call *me* dramatic?"

The outrage in his voice earned him another slight smile, complete with dimple, from Lee. Twinkling in humor, his hazel eyes morphed into the green of a dark forest. "Yes, and that should tell you something."

"It tells me you're going insane in there all alone."

Lee drummed his fingers on the other side of the door. Unlike before, they didn't land with dull thuds. Judging from the clicking noises, he'd grown his nails out into claws. Whatever weighed on Lee's mind would steadily crush him if left unchecked. Knowing that, Grant couldn't forget about him and run off to slake his lusts. This was his best friend for crying out loud.

"Look," Grant said. "I know you don't like to let anyone in when you're upset. If you like, we can sit together and watch the television. I won't ask any questions. But I'm not leaving."

"You won't give up, will you?" Lee asked, sounding tired.

"Nope."

The door shut with a thud. Moments later, the sliding lock came loose; the chain rattled as it swished back and forth across the wall. When Lee opened the door, his hazel eyes were an ominous brown—hard and defensive. He stood back, allowing Grant to come inside the room but not into his thoughts and feelings. Doing his best to remain cheerful in the face of Lee's temper, Grant said, "Permission to hug?"

"Permission granted, I suppose."

Was it Grant's imagination or did his friend lean into him a bit more than normal? For sure, he rubbed his hands in a small circle on Grant's back, which relaxed his sore muscles. Dammit, Lee was doing it again: sliding into the caretaker role instead of letting Grant comfort him.

"Come on, I'll give you a back rub," Grant said, pulling away. "Over to the bed."

At first, Grant thought Lee would protest. Indeed, his mouth stretched into a thin dissatisfied line, and tears, so odd for him, pooled in the corners of his eyes. Grant had promised no questions, but they lined up on his tongue and tripped over each other in a rush to get out. If he could uncover the source of Lee's torment, he could lift the burden from his shoulders and carry some of it.

"Oh, I recognize this. That's your sleuth-on-the-trail look. So pensive. So dashing. So...unwelcome right now."

"I gave my word—no more questions. I'll keep it."

"Oh, I know you will."

The sadness in the admission perplexed Grant. But he'd promised. He'd promised. He'd promised. And he'd keep his word.

Chapter Seven

Grant woke to being the big spoon to Lee's little, and he thought about how neatly they'd fit into the silverware drawer together. Trying his best to not wake his sleeping friend—while chanting *friend, friend, friend* to contradict the throb of his unhelpful boner—Grant untangled himself and carefully slid to the edge of the bed. No use. His weight dipped the mattress, rolling Lee forward against his butt. The warmth of his body pressed against Grant's, soothing his aching muscles. Until he met Lee, he'd always assumed vampires were cold creatures. They weren't. Their skin was soft, alive, and smelled like rain. Or maybe that was just Lee.

"Grant?" he said, blinking.

"Yeah, it's me. Get back to sleep."

"Did you...how long did you rub my back?"

"Until you fell asleep."

Groaning, Lee flipped around and looked at the clock. When he saw the hour was past midnight, he groaned again and wiped his face with his hands. His lips flapped as he blew out air. "Well, that's an entire day gone. Really, Grant, don't let my emo vampire crap ruin your time here."

"Emo vampire crap? Does this mean you're willing to talk to me now?"

"And if I say no?"

"Well, then my word is still good. We can go downstairs and grab a bite to eat. There are plenty of cute, sober humans who are willing to donate blood."

Lee snorted as though he didn't need to drink. Soon after, his stomach rumbled in disagreement. By now, he'd have to be damn near ravenous. Vampires couldn't go over two days without eating before they began to decompose, and he'd only barely sipped at the glass of blood he'd ordered this morning. His body must have been sapped of energy. The dark circles under his eyes certainly more than hinted at exhaustion.

Concerned for his friend, Grant dressed up the request as a plea. "Come on, I'm starving. Humor me. If you're worried you ruined my time here, it can be your treat."

"Yeah, I do owe you a beer or two, don't I?"

"You sure do."

Not really. But if taking care of Grant got Lee off the bed and to the bar, where he'd get the nourishment he needed, Grant could play the part of the aggrieved buddy whose vacation had been jeopardized.

"Oh, there's that look again. On the trail are we, dear heart? Don't deny it. I can practically see your nose twitching."

Grant smiled. "You got me. I'm worried about you."

"I'm fine. Brian showing his face surprised me. That's all. I assumed his aversion to vampires would keep him from anything like this."

"Yeah, his new squeeze said this was his last stint as undead. He was going to pull his fangs after."

Lee winced. "He seemed pretty green. Poor dove."

Nodding in agreement, Grant took a moment to absorb the new information. Earlier, he thought Lee might have known his ex would make an appearance. Drinking to excess wasn't Lee's style, but the behavior made sense if he'd been nervous about possibly running into Brian.

"Stop looking at me like that! I'm not a brain teaser!"

"That's exactly what you are, and you'll always blow my mind."

Lee's face twitched. Not quite a smile, not a frown, just an odd series of spasms Grant couldn't interpret, not without knowing more. But more details weren't forthcoming. Lee made that abundantly clear by going to the bathroom without saying another word. When the water turned on and Lee started to sing his favorite Queen song—"Don't Stop Me Now"—Grant leaned back on the bed for what would be a long wait.

To pass the time, Grant flipped through stations on the big-screen TV. Eventually, he settled on a haunted house show set in a sweeping mansion where each creak of the floorboards set the stage for the next jump scare. He was probably one of the few supernatural creatures who enjoyed each bump in the night and howl at the moon that came with Hollywood horror shows. Most other supernaturals saw them as low brow insults to their actual lifestyles and personalities.

When Lee, a towel wrapped around his waist and his wet chestnut hair sticking to flushed cheeks, sauntered into the room, Grant caught a whiff of his natural body odor intertwined with the lemony soap he used. Grant inhaled, rediscovering the old comforts of home. Odd how Lee's smell transported Grant back to the past, back to those memories where the two of them laughed all night and into the morning.

The moment Lee noticed what Grant was watching his scowl transformed into a huge grin. "You and your love for this shit."

"This one's a good one."

"You say that about them all. It's never true."

"So you say, but watch this…"

Lee plopped on the bed with a tired sigh and a flip of his hand toward the television as if to say, *I doubt this will be any different.* His naked skin brushed against Grant's shoulder, and for a second, his lemon scent carried Grant toward something new they could share rather than something old, but Grant had to brush the thought from his mind. Lee needed his rock after his bad breakup, not unwelcome pressure to embark on a new, risky romance.

The ghost, entangled in its past, floated across the screen on a mission to reclaim his hat from a boy thief. He pounded his cane on the floorboards—*tick, tick, tick, tick*—while the child huddled under the bed. His breathing, which he tried to slow to a steady pace, hitched in his throat.

Lee gasped and clutched his chest. "Oh my word, this is creepy shit."

"Yeah, told you."

"What's it called?"

"*The Haunting of Hill House.* Netflix."

Lee did a double take. "My word, they have that here?"

"Hulu too. This is a swanky place. Thanks for booking me a room here. I couldn't afford it on my salary."

Nodding, Lee sucked on his lower lip. His gaze darted all around the room, once again signaling some distress or mental dilemma Grant didn't understand and wouldn't be privy to anytime soon if Lee's stiff posture was any indication. Matters of the heart belonged to vampires, especially when it was the vampire's heart in question. Or so it seemed.

Lee slapped his knees. "Well, I cheaped out by booking the one room, so don't thank me too much. And I'm as fresh as I'm going to be. Time to go back to face the crowd."

Lee got dressed while Grant watched as much of the episode as time allowed. When he was ready, Lee said, "Good to go."

They walked shoulder to shoulder to the lobby. Lee's head hung low. His damp hair fell over his eyes, closing Grant off from reading his expression. Then and there, Grant vowed he'd break through if it was the last thing he did. Lee couldn't keep him out forever—promise or not. He had claws, too, and they were good for wall climbing.

Chapter Eight

Lee's color improved drastically after he drank. The sweet young thing in his arms sighed and nuzzled Lee's chin, biting softly at his neck. Eyes half closed as if on the brink of climax, he licked Lee's skin and muttered invitations, mixed with pleas, for more intimacy. Lee smiled indulgently at each offer and planted light kisses on the human's puckered lips.

The near pornographic scene wasn't an uncommon sight in the hotel's restaurant. Under the glittering light of crystal chandeliers and the muted jewel-colored aura of the stained glass, lovers kissed and groped each other. Only Grant—a hulking werewolf surrounded by an entire village of empty cheesecake plates—stood out in the crowd of blissful couples in various states of undress. Everyone who passed him said, "You must really love that cheesecake!" He didn't. It was something smooth and velvety to put into his mouth.

"Well, aren't we delicious," Lee said to the human wiggling in his arms. Wet and red with blood, his incisors puckered his bottom lip. Gently, he stroked the human's cheek, tucking a lock of his long blond hair behind his ear. Brown eyes open wide, lending him the appearance of a spring doe, the human fluttered his long eyelashes and ran his hand up Lee's stomach and then all the way to his neck.

Lee coughed into his fist. When Grant turned his way, he jerked his chin in the direction of the door, indicating Grant should beat it.

"Finally," the human said after Grant got up. "I want you all to myself."

Smiling impishly at the human's enthusiasm, Lee pointed at the young vampire, the guy with the tattoo and grunge band T-shirt, who'd offered himself to Grant earlier. "There's your ride," he said to Grant. "Have fun."

Cheesecake in hand, Grant snorted but left the lovebirds alone. Almost as soon as he flopped in the nearby booth, Lee and his doe-eyed beau started making out. Wincing at the wet smooching noises, Grant tried to console himself by remembering the human still didn't have a name. He meant nothing to Lee. They were here to have meaningless sex with willing strangers, not to meet their lifelong mates.

"You shouldn't care," Grant scolded himself.

"Or maybe you should," someone corrected him.

Grant hopped in his seat. Turning sharply, and expecting to see the tattooed vampire with the T-shirt Lee had pointed out, he began a polite refusal that died on his lips. Tattoo still lingered near the wall, watchful yet distant. The vampire who'd interrupted his private musings was far less ostentatious, even somewhat modest by vampire standards in his gray jeans and blue silk shirt unbuttoned to the navel. Each time he moved, Grant caught a quick glimpse of a perky nipple.

How the hell had anyone snuck up on him? Grant was a werewolf for crying out loud—sensitive hearing, smell, and tracking were supposedly his bailiwick. That aside, the vampire hadn't done much to conceal his movements. His cologne—expensive, judging by its subtlety—alone stuck out among the crowd. And he wore a necklace that had jangling dog tags. Grant ran his fingers through his hair and berated himself for getting so far off his game. Another day or two in the lap of luxury and he might end up getting bested by the rabbit he promised himself he'd hunt for a midnight snack.

The newcomer, who cheerily waved when Grant acknowledged him, fondled what appeared to be a cigarette package in his front pocket."I'm afraid I might have made a mistake. Werewolves are dangerous. One talking to himself...even more so."

Grant opened his mouth to respond but stopped short when a line of Lee's conversation with the human drifted in his direction. Sweet nothings, whispered in Lee's delicate voice, pounded as loud as a drumbeat into Grant's ear. Lee told the human his lips tasted like wine, his hair was the color of honey, and his eyes were dark pools of mystery. Okay, nothing between them seemed that serious. Those were throwaway lines, recycled from romance novels.

"Can I...can I sit?" the vampire asked.

Grant didn't know why he'd even want to anymore, but he'd been enough of an ass to say, "Please. And sorry about that. Please forgive me. What's your name?"

"Do we need names?"

"Well, it's easier if I have something to call you other than vamp."

The newcomer's lips twisted in a mischievous smirk reminiscent of Lee's. Actually, in a certain light, they shared a lot of characteristics. Both wore their chestnut hair on the longish side, letting it cascade in waves around their angelic faces. But the eyes were so different. This guy had warm brown, come-to-bed eyes with amber light flickering behind the curtains. Lee's were the aurora borealis.

"If it helps facilitate things, I'm going by Voldemutt."

"That's, uh—"

"My friend's joke name for me."

The vamp grinned. "The werewolf who shall not be named. I like it. You can call me Shelly."

Grant's brain registered the response, but it blanked on one of its own. The longer the silence stretched on, the more Shelly's eyes darted around the room. No matter how many times Grant told himself he was being boorishly rude, he couldn't get his mouth to cooperate to engage in light banter. He kept hearing threads of Lee's conversation; specifically, the coos and satisfied murmurs of the human he pleasured.

"You here as protection?" Shelly asked.

"No, no. Nothing like that."

"So you're here to hook up like everyone else?"

"I suppose I am."

"Well, you're doing a shit job of it, if you don't mind my saying so."

Grant gave the declaration, uttered so innocently in such a cloying baritone, a short bark of laughter. When the amber lights in Shelly's eyes danced in merriment, Grant finally thought of him as something other than a distraction. The wolf inside him licked its chops, and his heart—that damn heart of his—said, *Here he is, another one.* This time, he'd listen to the wolf. Screw his heart, the useless pattering thing that brought David after David into his life.

"Did you serve?" Grant asked, pointing at Shelly's tags.

"Yes. Two tours."

"Do you have your uniform?"

Shelly threw his head back and laughed. "That your thing, is it?"

"Tonight it can be, soldier. You into wolves?"

In response, Shelly tilted his head back and let out a low howl. Afterward, he searched around in the pockets of his tight jeans, which Grant looked forward to peeling off, until he found his hotel key. He tossed it onto the table. "Pick it up if you want me."

No more hesitation. No more sulking. No more of the loneliest-wolf-to-howl-at-the-moon routine. Grant threw a twenty on the table to cover the cheesecake he ate plus something extra for the worried waitress, who kept checking to see if he was about to stiff her. Earlier, he'd come across as the saddest sack in the room, so he supposed he couldn't blame her. He grabbed Shelly's key.

Grant breezed by the booth where Lee and his human companion locked lips. Lee broke away and gave Grant a quick glance and a lopsided smile.

"Dear heart," he mumbled into the human's ear. "Let's go upstairs."

Grant's guts twisted and he stopped in his tracks. Did he hear right? Had Lee called the human dear heart? Grant had always thought the endearment was specific to him, that Lee had no other in his life and never would. To think he said that to someone else—perhaps *everyone* else—brought on a whole wave of uncomfortable emotions.

"We still on?" Shelly asked and gave his hand a slight tug.

"Yes!"

Grant said it too loudly, with too much zeal. But it didn't matter. None of it did. Shelly wasn't here to meet his forever mate or even to remain with Grant beyond the end of their sexual encounter. So, Grant could be hung up on his ex, he could ignore Shelly's requests for conversation, he could even shout another man's name at climax. Whatever his body wanted. Nothing of what his heart needed.

Chapter Nine

Always five steps ahead, Lee had already pulled off his shirt. His body, lithe and graceful, glowed under the prismatic light of the overhead chandelier. He dared Grant to come to the bed where they'd grind their bodies until they both popped. He said, "Come on, don't be shy."

But it wasn't Lee. No. This vamp's name was Shelly, and he didn't have eyes like the aurora borealis; his were brown with amber highlights, lovely but not all the bright colors of the world swirled into one iris. While enticing, his smile didn't hint at an immortal lifespan worth of mischief, a vampire's allure. *No*, Grant's heart said. *No, no, no. This isn't what we want.*

Heat coiled in Grant's belly, setting fire to a passion he attributed to something—anything—other than his own thoughts. But he couldn't defeat his brain, electric with the possibilities of a forbidden courtship.

"Are we doing this?" Shelly asked.

Grant's heart thudded and crawled its way up to his throat, where it pitter-pattered its way to the top of his shit list. He combed his fingers through his thick black hair and tried to think of something witty. Uncertainty kept him tripping over his words until he was blurting out a whole stream of nonsense to drown in.

Brow furrowed in anger, Shelly said, "Okay, listen, you're obviously not into this, so I'm going to head out and find someone else."

As Shelly heaved his shirt back over his shoulders, Grant tried an apology he knew would fall on deaf ears. He'd earned it. Apparently, there were limits to the number of free passes he got in exchange for a night of meaningless, anonymous sex. Even the men with the lowest standards possible, the risk-seeking hookups who came here explicitly for passion lost patience with him.

"Sorry," Grant said again. "I know you're prob—"

"Yeah, yeah. Good luck with whatever it is you're doing here. Now get out of my room."

Grant left, muttering one last sorry as the door clicked shut. Soft as a breeze, Shelly said, "Sure thing, Limp Noodle."

And now he had a nickname he was certain would circulate among the crowd. Wishing he could shape-shift to match the wallpaper, Grant hung his head and counted tiles to keep from sprinting through the hall. His heavy footsteps clomped like the hooves of a warhorse. Ever since childhood, he'd been at odds with the environment, but he especially hated how his massive bulk stood out in the dollhouse halls of the expensive hotel.

"Coming back my way?"

Grant suppressed a jump and an expletive. Once again, he'd wrapped himself in a snare of his own thoughts and forgotten to keep his inner animal on call. Grant, happy no other werewolves came to the event, acted as though he'd detected the vamp's presence all along and was deigning to give him notice. When he recognized who it was—Tattoo, the hipster vampire wearing a grunge T-shirt—Grant offered a slight smile and an even slighter wave and tried to breeze past on his way to the lobby where there was cheesecake.

The vamp blocked him. Smiling big, his incisors resting on his lower lip, he waggled his eyebrows. "Knocking on someone else's door, or are you free for the rest of the night?"

"I'm..." What was he? Grant didn't know anymore. "I'm...on my way to the lobby?"

"Are you asking? If so, you've got a hall pass."

Laughing, more like wheezing awkwardly, Grant said, "Hey, thanks. I guess I'll use it."

Grant ducked his head and continued to plod along. Behind him, the reedy vamp hefted a sigh that probably weighed more than he did. "If you change your mind, I'm room number 205; come give me a call."

"Will do!" Grant shouted over his shoulder.

Heavy and uncooperative, Grant's feet carried him to a destination his brain only vaguely signed off on. He'd nixed the lobby idea in favor of another scheme, where he didn't spend the rest of his vacation alone and stuffing his gut with sweets until his waistband cried out for mercy. That could be a backup plan after all else failed.

A ding, followed by the sound of doors sliding open, indicated an elevator had stopped on his current floor. Grant trotted to beat the short window before the damn thing closed and left him to wait for five minutes until another one came along. Too late. The elevator, packed to the brim with vamps and humans standing shoulder to shoulder, closed its doors the moment he stepped foot in the adjacent hall. Spitefully, at least that's how Grant interpreted the elevator's normal functioning, the numbers lit up as it took its journey without him.

"You have to be kidding me," Grant said and slapped the wall with an open palm.

Nearby, the stairwell beckoned. Trying to focus on the bright side, Grant decided an alternate route would burn cheesecake calories and get his blood pumping. He didn't want to wear himself out too much, though, so he slowed to a light pace while he climbed to the fifth floor.

Before he could talk himself out of his madness, which is exactly what he should have done, Grant stood in front of the doorway to the room he shared with Lee. Two male voices—one moaning, the other whispering sweet encouragements— penetrated through the thick wood of the door. Grant flushed at the intimacy of the scene he imagined: tangled limbs, tongues, and bed sheets. But what had he expected? After all, Lee and the human he'd been with hit it off in spectacular fashion. They'd practically been banging it out in the cramped booth.

Grant's nerves frayed to strings as he questioned why he'd ever thought coming here was a good idea. Earlier, he'd imagined himself taking Lee's hand in his own and saying, "Everyone else came here to taste something forbidden. Why not us? We can have the fantasy and go back to normal. Lovers here, friends back home."

It made sense, didn't it?

At that exact moment, Lee belted out a long string of *oh yeses* as if agreeing but in a mocking way.

Grant slapped his cheeks to clear his head. A couple walking down the hall lingered near him, throwing suspicious stares over their shoulders and chatting about how odd he was to just stand there. Grant lifted his hand in a friendly wave, wincing when they only cocked their brows in response.

Going back to the lower level took considerably less time and effort. Grant let gravity do most of the work, only using his muscles to keep him from pitching face forward down the flight of stairs. In the lobby, a couple of vamps lounged on a plush velvet sofa and let loose a loud wolf whistle as he walked past. Grant ignored them and made a beeline straight for the door. When the cold night air hit his skin, hot from embarrassment, he let loose a sigh of relief.

"Fuck my heart," Grant shouted at a topiary shaped like an elephant. He especially hated it because its trunk stood long and erect, the way his dick should have been. "The miserable thing."

Chapter Ten

Bitter cold dry air nipped at Grant's exposed skin. He ran his hands up and down his muscular arms, coaxing the coarse hair there to stand on end, but, ultimately, his efforts yielded little result and he continued to shiver.

Fool that he was, Grant hadn't bothered to put on a jacket before bolting to the great outdoors, and if he had any sense left at all, he'd go back inside where it was warm. Instead, he removed his shirt and flung it to the ground and then savagely kicked the flimsy garment against the mocking elephant topiary. His pants followed. And his underwear. He'd been humiliated enough tonight; he wasn't going to prowl the woods as a wolf wearing boxers. He'd avoid that fate at the very least.

Standing naked, Grant allowed the wind to take deep, punishing bites from his flesh. He wiggled his toes, tinged with blue, and studied the tips of his fingers, which had taken on the same bruised color. He laughed out loud, recalling the series of bad decisions that had brought him to the woods for a vampire fête where the hookups were random and the heart played bench.

A door opening caught his attention. Soon after, voices—thin, high, drunk—floated to his ears. The female giggled at something her partner whispered and then whined about the bone-quaking wind leaking through the thin layers of her silken gown, which was almost as impractical as being naked.

To keep from getting caught wagging his front tail, Grant shifted to his wolf form. The thrill of transformation, the heightened senses that released him from the fragile shell of humanity, warmed his icy skin.

All at once, a bundle of new smells intermixed with the old to create a world of different possibilities. To his right, tiny fish swam in a shallow creek. Puny, not worth eating. To his left, a deer rummaged through the frozen foliage; its hooves clomped on the frozen ground. Too big, too much leftover carnage. Deeper in the forest, almost beyond the range of his heightened senses, vermin went in and out of their burrows.

Grant smelled rabbit. And then he remembered the promise he'd made himself.

Snow crunched under his feet, tracing his path so wary animals fled before he saw them. Other elements conspired against his purpose: the air billowed clouds of his breath, the ground surrendered the sound of his location, the white blanket of snow drew an arrow to his brown fur. Grant didn't mind. He enjoyed the extra challenge. Usually, his animal senses, combined with his human intellect, rendered such sport trivial.

Grant stayed low to the ground, keeping his head behind a snowdrift, his body perfectly still, and his golden yellow eyes fixated on the rabbit's burrow. Up ahead, a small brown dot hopped across the landscape, weaving in and out of the cover of the tree line and the openness of the glade. Beneath him, Grant's paws, instinctively eager for the thrill of a chase, twitched. He forced himself to remain closemouthed and motionless.

Grant risked taking another deep whiff of air. He smelled the rabbit, the deer, and the rot of decaying leaves. He smelled Lee? The last had to be a trick of his mind. Either that or Lee's scent, heavily saturated on Grant's discarded clothes, had imprinted itself onto his skin. Regardless, he didn't need the distraction.

Grant brushed his friend's enticing aroma into the things-I-can't-hunt bin where he stored an ongoing list of forbidden fruits unsuitable for his sharp teeth and carnivore diet. He couldn't control who shared Lee's bed, but he could control the hunt.

The rabbit. Where had it gone? Shit. Why did he keep losing touch with his animal side? The whole ordeal was more embarrassing now that he was actually in wolf form.

Grant perked up his ears, hoping to catch the steady beat of his prey's heart or at least the cleverly hidden patter of its footsteps. Nothing. Had he been able to curse as a wolf, an entire string of obscenities would have burst from his maw. Howling would most certainly tip off any lingering prey, so Grant swallowed his frustration and set to a longer wait.

Focus, Grant. Focus. Track its scent.

Ah, there it was—the rabbit. Relief drowned out Grant's fear of losing his touch with his inner animal. The notion had been absurd. He couldn't divorce himself from the wolf inside him anymore than he could peel off his skin and live. It was the only until-death-do-we-part relationship he might ever enjoy. He should marry the creature inside him and get a new toaster and some bath towels. Why the hell not?

Okay, Grant. That's the opposite of focusing.

The rabbit flicked one of its long ears. Nose twitching, the critter scanned for threats. Finding none, Grant had made sure to stay downwind, the rabbit took a cautious hop outside of his den and then a few more. Each second the skittish creature survived unmolested, it grew bolder until, finally, it turned its full attention to rummaging the dead land for any trace of food.

Wind tore through his fur as he bolted toward the helpless animal, which caught onto the chase too late. In its panic, it ran farther from the safety of its burrow. Grant, his muscles taut and adrenaline pumping through his veins, pounced as it darted for some underbrush. Beneath his paws, the creature struggled. Grant, teeth out and ready, lowered his head for the kill.

"Grant? That you?" Lee's voice was crystal clear in the otherwise muted forest. So Grant *had* smelled him earlier; he wasn't going crazy. That was a welcome revelation.

"Yeah, it's me," he answered after he shifted back to human form. The rabbit squirmed and squealed beneath him.

Lee floated toward him from above, touching down right at Grant's nose.

"You caught yourself a bunny there?" he asked, studying the scene with a cocked eyebrow and smiling lips, which were swollen from kissing. Grant swore he could sense the sarcasm before it dropped. When Lee tilted his head to the side, his tussled bedroom hair draping over his pale shoulder, Grant anticipated there'd be a playful bite in his voice before he said, "And here you are Elmer Fudding it in the forest while the rest of us hump like rabbits. What's the matter, dear heart? Vamps not to your taste?"

Grant lifted his hand and shooed his friend. "Better leave before this gets messy."

"Not going to happen. Give me that poor thing, you addict." When Grant failed to obey, he said, "Come on, come on, come on. I'll stand here all night and judge you."

Lee didn't make empty threats, so Grant, with a heavy sigh, stood and handed him the rabbit. "There, you happy?"

For a moment, Lee stood there taking stock of Grant's naked state. Perhaps it was his imagination, but Grant swore Lee's eyes darkened and his lips drew back from his sharp teeth as though he wanted to bite into something. After a long pause, he said, "I'm a vampire. Of course I'm not happy. Where are your clothes?"

"I shed them near the door. So, what are you going to do with that thing exactly?"

Lee pursed his lips as he thought. "Tell you what, you can have it back after you've bedded someone. Think of it as a reward for good behavior."

"It's terrified, you realize."

"Poor baby. Here, let me fix that."

Lee held the wide-eyed rabbit in front of his face. Large and dark, his pupils snared the creature in a trance as old and mystical as vampires themselves. Its rigid body relaxed in his hold, and its eyes glazed over. Soon, it rested in the nook of Lee's arm like a tame and lazy cat, nose twitching and ears flat on its head as if it had no cares in the world.

"Did you...did you glamour a rabbit?"

"Sure did. Now shift back to wolf and let's go inside. You can put some clothes on when we get to our room."

"Are you seriously going to store that thing in our room?"

"He's not a *thing*. And yes."

"It's a damn animal, Lee!"

"I *know*, Mr. *Wolf* with your big, pointy teeth."

Not knowing what else to do—arguing with Lee truly was a useless endeavor—Grant shifted back to his quadruped wolf form and loped behind as Lee hovered above the snow back to the hotel.

Curiously, Grant's clothes were no longer anywhere near the elephant topiary where he'd left them. Nearby, Grant caught the scent of the vampire who kept approaching him, the one with the come-hither tattoo. Intermixed with his familiar odor, a new potent one introduced itself—sunblock and a tangy cologne that was heavy on the alcohol.

Grant sneezed to dislodge the stench from his sensitive nostrils. Then, he thought no more of it.

Chapter Eleven

Grant, in Lee's thrall, became a fluffy pet intent on pleasing its stringent master rather than a majestic werewolf whose animal form struck fear into the hearts of men. Lee, who carried his ensorcelled rabbit the way socialites carried small dogs, didn't suffer from a similar diminishment. Through the lobby, up the stairs, and then through the hallway, he strolled with his head held high and his sarcastic wit ready to bite anyone who dared question his quirky tastes in companions. Indeed, he gave the impression that the vampires who weren't carrying rabbits and escorting werewolves—and that was all of them—were woeful creatures ill-suited to the modern world.

Once Lee closed the door to their hotel room, Grant shifted back to human form. Through lowered lashes, Lee scanned Grant's naked body, lingering on his half-erect cock. Grant mustered all his resolve to keep himself from going full stiffie under his friend's frank gaze. Another part of him thrilled at the chance to display his wares, wanting Lee to do a thorough job in his assessment and find Grant exceeded his standards. To be thorough, Lee'd have to use his hands, his mouth, his teeth.

After a while, Lee said, "At least your escapade didn't give you frostbite."

The offhand remark cut the wind out of Grant's sails. He'd been counting down the seconds while thinking

Lee's long pause might have hinted at something more intimate than merely checking for injuries and he was about to hear a declaration of a more personal nature. That didn't happen. Obviously.

Lee tossed the glamoured rabbit onto his bed and clucked in discontent when the thing let loose a slurry of butt pellets. Grant stifled a laugh that Lee, judging by his tightened grimace, heard.

"Sorry, but there is a drop of karma to it."

Lee chuckled. "Yeah, maybe. What do we want to name him?"

"*What*?"

In response, Lee pointed at the rabbit, which was stupidly hopping around on the bed sniffing and pawing at the covers in its eternal search for food. When that failed to yield results, the damn thing dug. By this time tomorrow, the rabbit might have itself a nice new burrow in the mattress and Grant would no doubt be the one sleeping on the floor.

Incredulous, Grant asked, "You want to name the thing I'm going to eat later?"

"We've talked about this. It's not a thing; it's a *him*. So, give me a male rabbit name—go."

Grant flipped his hands in the air. "Peter!"

"Original."

"Then you name it!"

With his head tilted to the side, Lee considered the vermin at length. He snapped his fingers. "Lucky. That way when I tell you to go get lucky, you'll have yourself two options."

"How sweet. I couldn't manage without you."

"I *know*!"

Their gazes met. The aurora borealis flickered in Lee's eyes, making it impossible for Grant to stay mad at him even though he'd ruined his dinner plans and coaxed him into taking a vacation that Grant had known was a mistake the moment he got into the car. No matter what type of nonsense mischief Lee concocted in his neurological laboratory, Grant swallowed the mad science that resulted. It was a ride he went on again and again even though, again and again, it went nowhere.

Grant asked, "Did you enjoy your time with Unnamed Human?"

"I did!"

"Really? He seemed...odd."

"Well, that's me. When I find myself a unicorn, I have to ride it."

Grant coughed out an uneasy laugh he hoped masked his discomfort.

Lee raised his eyebrow. "How about you? Did you manage to snare anything other than Lucky?"

Grant coughed again and turned to hide his face, which flushed with embarrassment. A variety of tall tales—one where he was a sexual god rather than the guy who'd fled to the forest to chase a different sort of tail—stuttered on his lips. Nothing that would make him feel cool sprang to mind, so he kept quiet and hoped Lee, who sometimes flitted topic-to-topic like a well-dressed hummingbird, would move on.

"I'll take that as a no," Lee said. "What advice did I give you?"

"Fuck anything that moves?"

"Yes, that. Why aren't you doing that?"

Grant struggled to cobble together a lie that sounded truth-ish. To pull it off, he'd have to keep facing away from

Lee's keen eye. The moment he saw Grant, he'd discern the truth from his open-book features.

Grant fussed with the blanket, pulling and twisting the edges. While he made a show of getting ready to sleep, he gave a spiel that he hoped would throw Lee off the trail. At the very least, get Grant out of discussing his sexual failures and how his stupid heart showed up to throw him under the bus whenever he ventured too far into using-his-dick to-make-decisions territory.

"I'm not buying any of it," Lee said, interrupting Grant's explanation. "You're the worst at lying. Avoiding my eye—dead giveaway."

"Okay, okay. Today was...well, my name is now Limp Noodle."

Lee placed his hand on his chest. "Oh, dear heart."

"Yeah."

"What on earth did you do to earn that particular moniker?"

"Failure to perform."

Lee stuck his finger straight in the air and then crooked it. "Like that?"

Grant held up his finger and crooked it to mirror Lee's. "More like this...and just this."

"That's unfortunate. Dare I ask what happened? I sure hope it wasn't about Dave. That little twerp shouldn't plug anyone's works."

What was Grant going to say? That his heart was fantasizing about Lee, his best friend, instead of focusing on the task at hand? No, he'd promised Lee he'd never blur that line, and it was clear Lee booked the single room because of Brian; he needed emotional support from a friend, not seduction. Grant would remind himself of this fact however many times it took.

Grant said, "Yeah, I guess I'm not over him yet. You know, I'm just always so...so..."

"Fluffy?"

"Only *you* say so."

In response, Lee tossed one of the decorative pillows against his bed and snarled when it bounced and landed on the floor, cursing and kicking at it for good measure.

"You okay?" Grant asked, drawing back from the strange scene.

"Great!"

"*Obviously.* Goddamn."

"I'm fine. Really."

"You sure about that? The stuffing all over the floor is whispering something else in my ear."

"Yeah. Yes. I'm fine. I just get so pissed when I think of you stressing over David." Lee stuck his finger in the air again as if accusing the ceiling of high crimes and possible misdemeanors. "That nitwit is not worth losing an ounce of sleep over. He should have loved you better and kept your tender heart in a safe box."

Grant chuckled. "He'd have to rip it out first either way."

"Oh, you know what I mean."

They studied the rabbit—Lee on one side of the room, Grant on the other. The simple-minded creature, oblivious to Lee's temper tantrum, twitched its nose and flicked its long ears. Then, the critter flopped down on the bed and slept. Tummy grumbling, Grant settled in to do the same.

Eventually, Lee pressed against him, flooding Grant's body with a warmth both familiar and achingly distant.

Chapter Twelve

Grant woke to a fate worse than he expected. Breakfast—a bagel and a buttery ham omelet that melted in his mouth—constituted the highlight of his morning. Afterward, and almost immediately, he regretted crawling out of bed.

Brian, Lee's ex, had invited himself to the table and sat across from them with his arm slung over his sweet but vacant boyfriend, Cherub, who Grant assumed would eventually give his real name. Truly, he hated to see Cherub in love with someone as obviously possessive and manipulative as Brian, but there wasn't anything to do other than offer support to the young vampire who seemed, as Lee had said, as green as a sapling.

Lee, his aurora borealis eyes ablaze in anger, tapped his pointed nails on the tabletop. Judging by the growing shadow along his brow, he was about two seconds away from clawing out his ex's eyes. To Grant's relief—he didn't relish the idea of a full-scale battle in the middle of a hotel restaurant—Lee remained quiet and listened at least semipolitely.

Oblivious to the hostility, or simply not caring about it, Brian prattled on about his and Cherub's new life together once Cherub had his fangs pulled.

Blinking his big blue eyes, Cherub added, "It's like Romeo and Juliet. We'll die together."

"How sweet," Lee drolled. More genuinely, he added, "If that's what you want, I'm happy for you."

"Of course it's what he wants!" Brian said. "Why wouldn't he?"

Cherub, his eyes unreadable, nodded. "It'll be a whole new life for us."

Brian placed his hand over Cherub's and squeezed. Looking directly at Lee, he said, "Some don't understand the sacrifices love demands. They'd rather keep their fangs and spend time with limp noodles."

Lee shot up from the table and left. The chair he'd been sitting in clattered to the floor, attracting the attention of nearly everyone in the restaurant. A hundred heads—slight exaggeration—turned to ogle the scene. Shock turned to amusement as they studied Grant's flushed face. He had a pretty good idea what each smirk meant: Limp Noodle, the werewolf who couldn't get it up or get it on. He may as well go back home to face the social media disaster of being a monster.

"Excuse me, please," Grant said, keeping his voice level for Cherub, who appeared genuinely befuddled by the sudden turnaround in the conversation.

"Maybe we'll catch you one of these days for dinner?" Cherub said. He glanced at Brian to see if he agreed.

"Maybe so, and good luck in your new life," Grant responded.

It wasn't difficult to find Lee once Grant set himself to the task. All he needed to do was follow the scent of Twizzlers, Lee's favorite sinful comfort food. During Halloween, he'd sometimes stick them in his mouth and let the red rope candy dangle on his chin. To the children at the door he'd say, "I've sucked so much blood tonight, but I vant to suck *yours*!" The first few years hadn't gone over well, and Grant consigned himself to the task of calming terrified children as they ran from his yard screaming. Nowadays, parents knew what to expect and prepared their offspring accordingly.

Grant chuckled at the memory. In retrospect, he probably should have stopped inviting his friend over, due to his shenanigans, but it wouldn't have been Halloween without him.

He was smiling when he stumbled upon Lee, who was leaning against the wall, a Twizzler in one hand and an unlit cigarette in the other. Clucking his tongue, Grant prepared a light admonishment. Smoking, even for vampires, was a health risk, and Lee had been the one to break Grant of his habit, so he knew better.

"This is a no smoking zone, sir," Grant told him.

"It's not lit," Lee responded. "Go patrol elsewhere."

"I'm afraid not, sir. I'll need you to come with me back to the bar."

The surly lip curl Lee cast his way didn't deter Grant from his efforts. If anything, the glower strengthened his resolve to intervene to end his friend's sour mood. Maybe together they could salvage this train wreck of a vacation. They'd accomplished greater and lesser miracles when working as a team.

Grant wrapped his big arms around his friend and lifted him off the ground. Easily, because a vampire weighed next to nothing to a shifter, Grant slung Lee over his shoulder and rotated his body so that his head hung toward the floor. Lee's chestnut hair tickled the carpet.

Dry as butterless toast, Lee said, "What's this about exactly?"

"I'm turning your frown upside down."

"This is a never-ending hell."

"Yes, and I won't be able to survive it without you."

"I *know*. Story of your life."

Grant risked peeling off one of Lee's shoes. Daringly, he grabbed the pinky toe through his sock. "And this one went wee, wee, wee all the way home."

"I'm going to suck you dry."

Grant shuddered at the thought. Not out of fear. Nope. His limp noodle twitched, growing a bit more al dente in the confines of his tight clothes he'd picked to show off his assets. Happily, Lee's knees couldn't detect the sudden and unwelcome change in Grant's body, but Grant would have to stall until the episode passed. Lee was bound to notice the bulge.

When he trusted himself to speak, Grant said, "I thought this was how vampires like to sleep."

"Put me down, you giant dummy. And don't generalize about my species, you hairy buttsniffer."

"I sniff hairy butts?"

"You know what I meant! And probably. At least whenever you go to a family reunion. Now, seriously, put me down."

Well, Grant landed himself in quite the jam. His erection hadn't subsided. Quite the opposite. He'd progressed from limp to uncooked the more Lee verbally lashed him at the whipping post. At this rate, his dick would get so hard it would snap off in his trousers, which would make him a half noodle. He really wished the whole pasta thing never took root in his mind. Trying to run with the metaphor himself wasn't making it any better.

"Grant...?"

"Yeah...what?"

"You're still holding me upside down."

"Yeah. Right. Sorry about that."

"Sorry enough to, I dunno, put me down?"

Flinching from the steel in Lee's voice, which he'd stab in the gut if Grant weren't careful, Grant contemplated his predicament. Sooner or later, he'd have to do as Lee asked and let him go. Once on his own feet, Lee would have full view of Grant's body's most recent betrayal and it was a doozy. Doing his best to appear calm—totally in control, here—Grant plopped Lee onto the floor and fled.

"Wh—where are you going?" Lee shouted after him.

"Forgot something!"

"Are you running in the hall?"

"Trotting!" Grant corrected. "Running is against the rules!"

And he was breaking a lot of rules recently. Him, an ex-cop decorated for his strict adherence to the law and service to his community. The boundaries Lee put in place a long time ago—along with proper hall etiquette—should be respected and upheld. He was being a bad, bad dog. That's what he told himself as he flung open the door to storm into the hotel room.

He threw scalding hot water in his face to let it burn off the shame. Instead, his skin flushed an even more embarrassed shade of red and his cheeks tingled, sensitive to the touch. "Okay," he told his reflection. "Time to sort out your shit. You can contemplate your next move while you enjoy yourself a nice rabbit."

Grant stumbled out of the bathroom into the main sleeping area. The makeshift cage where they'd left the rabbit—two dressers pushed against the wall in a V-shaped barrier, was empty. Someone had broken into his and Lee's room and only left behind the stench of sunblock and cologne, the same scent that lingered around his clothes the night he'd gone hunting. Lucky, the rabbit, was gone.

Chapter Thirteen

Unlike Grant's mood, the forest had partially thawed in the afternoon sun, dim but powerful behind a veil of thin clouds. His feet squelched in the half-frozen mud, leaving behind shallow prints. Jagged thin shreds of ice clung at the outer edges, which curled like snarling lips. Later, the sky would clear, the moon would rise, and the ground would harden. Then, Grant would hunt himself a new rabbit. In the meantime, he'd search for the deadmeat—a not-so-nice term Grant used for vampires who'd pissed him off—who stole the last one.

"Hey, it's Limp Noodle out enjoying the sun," a vampire reclining under a black umbrella and the shade of a tall tree said. Beside him sat a beautiful woman with a cascade of curly brown hair; she popped grapes into her mouth and tittered at the jab. The vampire added, "Going to go catch us some fish with your trouser worm?"

Grant sniffed the air, hoping the sarcastic idiot would prove to be the thief so he could justify shifting to wolf form and chasing him for a touch of sport. No such luck. This wasn't his guy. He bit back, "No, I'm going to find the motherfucker who stole my rabbit."

They both laughed so boisterously at his declaration that he regretted ever saying it. Oh well. Not like his humiliation could get any worse. Four more days and he'd be on his way home where his entire precinct plus everyone he knew on social media would barge into his private life, ripping his dignity—at least what remained of it—to shreds. There'd be emails, tweets, and probably quite a few persistent gossips who'd show at his house to ask him for the personal details of his breakup with David. He couldn't stay hidden forever.

Light wind rustled the collar of Grant's shirt, throwing Lee's scent in his face on top of everything else. His cock bobbed, pressing against the fabric of his jeans. *Ding-dong,* it said. *Answer the door.*

"Would if I could, buddy," Grant said. "Would if I could."

Around him, the sound of social chitchat mixed with the forest's normal static of creaking wood, winter birds chirping as they flitted branch to branch, and the chattering of squirrels that checked and rechecked their stashes of food buried here and there. Beneath it all, the heartbeat of the creek pattered, sluggish in the cold but trying to push forward nonetheless. Grant focused on its signature and did his best to imitate its determination.

He stopped and took in another deep breath. The scent, a heavy mix of sunblock and a cheap grocery store cologne, he'd been trailing ended here but there were no other markers to indicate another's presence—either now or in the past. No footprints, no broken branches, no discarded objects. Also, no rabbit.

Grant swiveled his head left and right, trying to find a clue to chase before his own helplessness drove himself insane. The rabbit, he'd told himself, was something he could fix. Not David. Not Lee. But tracking prey came to him as naturally as the dog paddle. Sooner or later, he'd have the culprit. Afterward, he'd have a snack.

He took in a deeper breath and smelled...Lee?

"Hey there, dear heart." Lee wafted down from the sky holding a black umbrella looking like some sort of diabolical Mary Poppins. Cloaked from head to toe in dense fabric, he kept the sun at bay through clever outfit design. Always graceful, his fingers fluttered as he waved a cheery hello. "What are you doing out here? You better say getting laid."

"Looking for Lucky."

"That's not the same as getting lucky."

"You caught me not following your advice again. Good work."

Lee sniffled in indignation. He didn't make so much as a sound as he landed. During their friendship, Grant had taught him how to move quietly, masking his steps and thinning out his breathing so that only the most cunning and skilled hunters would detect him. Of course Lee used the acquired skills to play pranks and make Grant's life difficult.

Lee lifted an eyebrow. "Are you really going to do this?"

"What's that?"

"Hunt for your missing bunny instead of enjoying the party?"

"And how did *you* know the rabbit is missing?"

Lee shook his head to hide a taunting smile that reminded Grant of a smug cat's twitching tail. "Word spreads fast. You know what they're calling you now?"

"Go on, tell me."

"Wererabbit, as in where's my rabbit!" Lee laughed so hard his fangs popped out of his gums and droplets of his spittle splashed on Grant's face.

"Very droll. Are you going to help me or not?"

"Or not. Let's go back to the hotel and grab a bite to eat. The sun is not good for my undead complexion; the umbrella only blocks so much. Do you want me to singe out here?"

Honestly, kind of. But then that wasn't fair. Lee didn't know how much his mere presence tormented Grant. He wished that he'd never thought about the possibility of them being together. The whole fantasy, something he couldn't pass off as a spur of the moment whim when he continually longed for a mere brush of the shoulder from the off-limits Lee, had been a bad idea. Now, Grant couldn't escape; the claws of it dug straight into his heart and squeezed so hard Grant swore he could taste blood in his throat.

"Well?" Lee asked. "Are you coming?"

"No, I'm going to solve this thing."

"Oh, you're too cute when you go into supersleuth mode."

Grant waved Lee away and hoped his friend would take the hint and bugger off before Grant snapped and either pulled Lee into his arms or pushed him away, emotionally or physically. Instead of leaving, Lee sighed dramatically, rolling back his thin shoulders as though he were about to set himself to an unpleasant task and needed to muster all his strength.

"Seriously, go on inside," Grant told him. "Save your fair complexion."

"No, no. Let Lee solve your problems. So, you want to find your bunny thief, huh?"

"That's the idea."

"Well, who are the usual suspects?"

Grant lifted his eyebrow. Whenever Lee tried to play detective, he referenced the most popular cop movies, shows, or books. Media rarely accurately portrayed how real investigations ran and had a tendency to glorify macho cops, and it annoyed Grant whenever people would judge the value of his work based on what Clint Eastwood did in *Dirty Harry*. Not that Grant's current undertaking, finding some schmuck who'd stolen his rabbit, constituted a real investigation. He was going off-the-cuff with this one.

"I can't exactly round up suspects, Lee. This isn't an investigation. This is more like...well..."

"Wasting time?"

"Yes. That."

"Well, then, I'm extra qualified help."

The mischievous glint in Lee's eye spoke to the truth of the statement. Yet, Grant thought of the task as a solo venture, where he focused on something to fix, rather than a dynamic duo type of situation. He needed to get his head clear. Having Lee hovering over his shoulder, breathing on the back of his neck, wouldn't help in that particular matter.

Grant waved Lee off again, gesturing for him to go back to the luxurious hotel where he could find all sorts of amusements. "We came here to have fun. I'm being a—"

"*Total* drag?"

"Yes."

"So, let's solve this rabbit thing and get back to what we came here to do. Huh?"

Grant never found it in himself to say no to Lee's expression—the curling lips that showed just a hint of fang, all the lights in his eyes dancing with glee, and the somewhat predatory crinkle in his nose. God, he got everything he wanted with that face.

"I couldn't make it without you," Grant said.

"I *know*. Believe me, I know."

Chapter Fourteen

A thick canopy umbrella shielded Grant and Lee from the harsh rays of the sun–keeping Lee from disintegrating and Grant from panting. The horse pulling their carriage through the hotel's park let loose a stream of poo, which plopped on the freezing ground and steamed. Its hooves clanked on the gravel path, thudding loudly enough to helpfully drown out the beat of Grant's heart as Lee's hand rested casually, as if it belonged there and nowhere else, on Grant's knee. The weight of it served as a constant reminder of his traitorous urges to woo his best friend.

Grant had flagged down the carriage driver on impulse. Earlier, while he'd stalked around the hotel grounds, he'd noticed other couples merrily taking the ride–some of them holding bouquets of flowers–and laughing at raunchy jokes or playful bits of gossip. To his eye and ear, they'd appeared blissfully happy.

Grant told himself the carriage provided him with a favorable vantage point for his investigation and that's why he'd decided to hop in for a ride. His quarrelsome heart stuttered in disagreement. It told him he'd wanted to make a romantic gesture toward Lee; the whole rabbit thing provided a convenient excuse.

Shut up, heart.

Lee pinched his nose. "I guess I don't get the appeal of this. I'm seeing the same park from a slightly higher elevation and there's a foul-smelling animal in front of me. Also, beside me." Lee sniffed Grant's shoulder. "Yuck. Wet dog."

"Ha, ha. You're such a funny guy," Grant said.

"You deserved the jab. Stop saying we're looking for deadmeat. It's offensive to vampires."

"Fine. I'll say we're searching for a necrofella. Get it?"

"That's not better. You're being downright dastardly rather than dashing." He wagged one of his fingers in Grant's face. "That's not a good look on you."

Grinning ear to ear, Grant wiggled his eyebrows and let loose his best straight-from-a-comic-book evil cackle. He tapped the tips of his fingers together for added villainy. All he needed was a black cloak and a creepy animal sidekick, preferably a white cat that would purr on command, to complete the effect.

"That's just unsavory. You're supposed to be the hero in the story."

Grant's heart fluttered. Did he say hero? If so, did that mean Lee thought of him as one in general or as *his* hero? And dashing. Lee called him that too. He'd heard that right. The possibilities swirled around in Grant's head like dollars in a money booth, and he grabbed at them with the greedy zeal of someone grasping for a fortune.

"And there you go. Off to space."

"Sorry," Grant said. "A lot on my mind."

Lee frowned. "David again?"

That was much safer than discussing the actual trajectory of his thoughts, the absolute clusterfuck nightmare path his heart set him to wander. "Yeah. Yes. Sorry, trying to do better and not think about the breakup. I dread going back home to face the accusations. You know, the endless questions about what happened, and did I really turn into a monster and chase David around my yard? That type of thing."

"Right. That is going to suck."

"Good way to put it."

"Need my help?"

"I'll give you a call if I need someone to make sarcastic remarks and make things so much worse."

Smacking his lips, Lee made a point to appear affronted, but the lights dancing in his eyes undercut the illusion. Although it was at his expense, Grant enjoyed his friend's playful amusement, so welcome after his morose temper at the start of their vacation. Seeing him smile again, especially when it was genuine, brought a happy grin to Grant's face too. He almost forgot about the rabbit, not to mention the whole mess of potholes surrounding his personal life that he'd have to sidestep.

Lee, his voice quivering, said, "Grant?"

"Hmm?"

"A monster isn't something you can turn into. Either you are or you aren't. And you most definitely are not. You have the teeth, not the chops."

The odd speech, delivered in a hushed whisper that Grant strained to hear, ended when Lee flipped his hands in the air. Rolling his eyes as if he'd just said something ludicrous and expected a glib response in return, Lee regarded Grant through lowered lashes in a manner one might confuse with shyness. But that word and his friend mixed like water and oil, so Grant shook the thought out of his head.

Grant used his elbow to poke Lee in the ribs. "I'm mostly fluff. Right?"

"You are. Yes. And don't say I'm the only one who will ever think so. Your self doubt is tedious."

"Sorry my personal issues tax you so. I put you through too much."

"I *know*."

"Tell me, do you think I'll escape this place with fewer than four embarrassing nicknames?"

Lee considered his question for all of a split second before answering. "Doubtful. At this rate, you'll be everyone's favorite punch line. I think you're already trending as a meme on Twitter even though no one here has access to the internet. Your quirky behavior transcended the boundaries of reality, and vampires, like life in Jurassic Park, found a way."

"You could have said that I'd be fine."

"Well, you'll always be fine, but your image as an animal sex machine is officially over."

"Harsh."

Quirking his eyebrow in a way he normally reserved for when Grant cheated at cards, Lee frowned at the response. "I must say...for a PI, you're really bad at following the clues."

Grant craned his neck, scanning the area for potential clues that he might have missed. He didn't see, hear, or smell anything out of the ordinary. "What's that? You notice someone behaving suspiciously?"

Sighing, Lee said, "Nothing. Everything is fine, fine, fine. Note the emphasis on the word." He drummed his fingers on his knee, indicating he had more to say. Grant patiently waited, knowing his friend hated interruptions. Finally, he practically blurted, "My name for you is fluff-a-luff-a-gus."

"Is that a play on Mr. Snuffleupagus? The Sesame Street mammoth?"

"You got it. Did you know he was so ginormous that two actors had to play him?"

Grant didn't know for sure; he wasn't much of a television show buff, but he could have assumed the massive puppet wasn't easy to handle. What surprised him was that Lee knew so much about a kid's program known for its breezy optimism and its focus on teaching moral lessons. Lee wasn't some depraved monster. It's just he was the type to stick ropes of Twizzlers in his mouth and tell children it was blood trailing down his chin. But only on Halloween.

Laughing, Grant said, "And are you Big Bird?"

"Why on earth would you say that?" Lee cackled and pulled up his pants. "Is it my chicken legs?"

"No, no. Because he was the only one who could see Snuffle. Wasn't that Big Bird? Or am I remembering wrong?"

"No, that's right. But, as Martin Robinson said, 'He's not invisible. He just has bad timing.'"

"Jesus, is that really a line in the show?"

Lee nodded.

"Please tell me you can't remember the episode number."

In response, Lee sucked in air and lifted his shoulders in an apologetic shrug.

"No way."

"Afraid so."

"Look at me riding in a buggy with Count Nerdula."

"I liked Count Karaoke better," Lee said and gave his shoulder a gentle slap. "But you can call me whatever you like, I suppose. That's the privilege of being you."

Lee gave him another sideways glance, raising his eyebrow as though he were a director and Grant was an actor who should be saying his lines. Was this some type of test, a dare, a secret wish? Grant met Lee's eyes and channeled all his hopes into the last option, but Lee stayed tight-lipped, silent against the efforts of Grant's pleading heart.

Chapter Fifteen

During the totally not-intended-to-be-romantic carriage ride, they'd turned off the beaten path and set a new course on a gravel pathway that went deep into the woods. The clip-clop of the horse's hooves kept time to the pitter-patter of Grant's heart. The tree line of the towering evergreens and red alders, along with the carriage's checkered fabric canopy, provided enough shade for Lee to doff layers of clothing.

Grant opened his big mouth and prepared to hear an indignant response to the stupid question he was about to ask. "What are the other advantages—?"

A sudden loud crack of splintering wood cut Grant off midsentence. Their driver, a sullen man who'd barely said five words since he spouted a scripted greeting, burst out a string of expletives.

Grant and Lee pitched forward in their seats, then, just as suddenly, tilted to the side as the cab of their carriage skidded to the ground. In a flash, Grant—hoping his mass would absorb the impact—positioned his body to cushion Lee's fall. His friend's limbs tangled in his as they hit the ground. Above them, the carriage lay on its side, rocking dangerously on the gravel pathway.

The tethers attaching the horse to the carriage broke, and the beast made a run for the woods.

"Grant! The sun! I don't sparkle! I singe, and I *hate* it."

Of course, they'd tipped over in one of the few clear patches of road where the sun shone full blast. Nearby, spots of shade mocked their piss-poor luck, symbolic of the entire trip so far.

The brightly checkered umbrella that had shielded Lee from the harmful ultraviolet rays came loose in the tumble. The wire meshing underneath had bent in the crash, twisting the fabric into an unhelpful clump of wire and webbing. Earlier, when they'd begun the ride, Lee had shed his layers of clothes in favor of a simple T-shirt. Parts of the discarded outfit were scattered nearby.

Grant transformed and flung himself on top of Lee. As the weight of the carriage smashed on top of them, Grant lifted one of his massive paws to deflect the blow. Pain shot up through his arm, spreading like fire through his chest until the entire upper half of his body flared in protest. A low whine escaped from his throat, but Grant forced himself to lift upward, tilting the buggy until it rolled back on its side.

Their driver, sitting on his butt with his hands splayed out behind him, studied Grant with open-mouthed wonder. As a human, he probably hadn't ever seen a werewolf in its upright form. To keep people from freaking out, as well as for logistical reasons related to travel, most of Grant's kind kept to four legs.

After waving in what he hoped was a friendly, not sinister way, Grant gestured to Lee's hoodie and his discarded umbrella.

"You...you want those, big fella?"

Grant nodded.

Beneath Grant, Lee snorted. Grant would have done the same but feared any noise might startle the already agitated driver, who was supposedly hired due to his experience with the supernatural. So far, he hadn't run away screaming with his hands above his head, which made him a better date than anyone Grant had ever had a long-term relationship with. Perhaps later, assuming Lee didn't burn to a crisp, Grant would hunt down the young man and try to make a go at it.

Yeah, that's a terrific idea, his heart told him. *It'll be just like getting with—*

Shut up, heart.

"Fella?" the driver asked. Crouched on the ground, he stayed as far away from Grant as he could possibly manage. He gripped Lee's hoodie in his fist and gestured as if he was about to throw it. Grant nodded again, holding up his hands to indicate he was ready to catch.

The human, his sides heaving in and out as though he'd run seven miles uphill, tossed the hoodie and then scurried back to the tree line on the other side of the gravel path. His gaze darted to Grant, to the carriage, and to the forest as though he couldn't quite make up his mind if he wanted to do his job or flee the scene.

"He...he okay?" the driver asked. His lower lip trembled.

Lee, his voice muffled, said, "Great! Thanks for asking!"

Grant heaved a massive sigh as he tried to get Lee back into the protective confines of his clothes. Due to his claws, he fumbled with the heavy fabric, delicate in his paws and prone to ripping apart. In short, he was doing a pretty shit job of things while Lee, impatience radiating from his coiled body, waited.

"For hell's sake, just transform back to human," Lee eventually said.

But then Grant would be naked and Lee would be underneath him. Like, his mouth might be right next to Grant's cock. How could he possibly—

Lee interrupted his thoughts. "Did you hear me? Grumble for yes."

Grant grumbled.

"Then shift!"

Dreading what his body's reaction might be, Grant shifted back to his human form. To his relief, his cock remained flaccid between his legs, for now, but he didn't know how long he could maintain his resolve with the tip pressed against Lee's stomach. Thinking about it wouldn't help, so Grant set himself to counting to twenty billion, that oughta do it, while Lee squirmed beneath him.

Lee took a sharp breath that Grant associated with pain.

"Were you singed?"

"N...no."

"What's wrong?"

Lee's stomach brushed against the tip of Grant's dick. "I...I'm...uh...I'm."

"Jesus, are you okay?"

He wiggled again. "*Yes*! Are you going to help me get the hoodie over my head or not?"

Large enough to cast Lee in shadow, his human body acted as a barrier against the harmful UV rays, so Grant wanted to remain protectively coiled over his vulnerable friend for as long as possible. But, Lee was right; he hadn't managed to squirm back into his clothes on his own. At least he hadn't been able to accomplish much in the minute since Grant slid the shirt to him.

"Okay, give me the hoodie. Good. Now, when I move, lift your hands above your head. You ready to do this?" Grant asked.

"Yeah. On three."

They counted down together. "One, two, three."

Quickly as he could, which made him a bit rough, Grant shoved the hoodie over Lee's head and then pulled down on the hem until Lee's head poked through. Disheveled, and electric with static, his crown of chestnut hair flew everywhere until Grant jerked up the hood, containing it. Strands of hair still clung to his puffing cheeks, which billowed in and out. All the colors of his borealis eyes flickered as though his brain was trying to process everything that had happened.

"Any sun damage?" Grant asked.

Lee checked himself all over. "I don't think so. I think I made it." To the driver, he shouted, "What the hell was that?"

The driver wrapped his arms around his knees. "I don't know. This hasn't ever happened before."

"Helpful."

Grant put his hand on Lee's shoulder and pulled back before his friend stalked over to the young man, who looked at them in wide-eyed wonder as if they'd magically appeared. Grant didn't quite understand. The event had been sudden and unexpected, but not as traumatic as the young man's behavior would suggest. Then, to a human, the carriage crash might have been far more horrifying.

"Stay here," Grant told Lee. "I'm going to go talk to him."

Lee pursed his lips. "Okay, I'm going to give the carriage a look over. Figure out what his deal is if you want."

Chapter Sixteen

Grant thought about chasing after Lee to ask him if he was upset with something other than the wreck, but he ended up going over to their driver instead because dealing with a traumatized human seemed safer than messing with a vampire who'd nearly been singed. Especially when that vampire was Lee. Plus, his nude state didn't lend itself to a buddy-buddy conversation. His cock was bound to barge into that chat with plenty to say.

Gravel dug into the thin flesh of Grant's feet. As he gingerly trudged forward, he stopped to scrape loose rocks out of his flesh. A few had bored their way through and left deep welts, which bled and stung. He chastised himself for not putting on his heavy-duty, thick-soled boots, which might have at least partially survived transformation. Then, he hadn't expected to shift. This whole trip hadn't gone according to plan.

"You going to be okay—" Grant squinted at the driver's nametag. "—Fredrick?"

"Yeah, yeah."

"Can you walk?"

"I... I think so. Are you...your arm...is it...hurt?"

"I'll heal fast. Shifter advantage."

Fredrick nodded dumbly and gulped. His eyes met Grant's then darted away like minnows. After another big gulp, he asked, "Where's...where's Ned?"

"Who?"

"The horse," Lee yelled from a distance. "He ran off into the forest."

Fredrick blinked. "We need to go find him. I'm going to be in so much trouble. My boss loves that horse."

Grant perked up his ears and scanned the nearby area for any sign of the missing animal, but only the chirping of birds and the babbling creek, which had thawed some and rushed forward nearly unhindered, caught his attention. While Grant searched, Fredrick, in a manner Grant was sure he thought inconspicuous, took stock of Grant's naked body. Flushing, he covered his face and turned away. Such modesty amidst a vampire fete amused Grant. He wondered where the blushing Fredrick went when couples were literally screwing in the hallways.

"What's going on here?" Lee asked, scowling at them from beneath his dark hood.

Grant flashed what he hoped appeared like an apologetic smile. "We have to find Ned."

"I'll only agree because I'm an animal lover, but you need to come over here and take a look at the carriage first. I don't think this was an accident."

"You going to be okay without me?" Grant asked Fredrick. When the man nodded, Grant rose and turned to Lee. "Show me."

The trek back to the carriage was every bit as excruciating. This time, the rocks bore into the previous wounds—going deeper than before. By the time he got back to the hotel room, his feet would need a lot of TLC. Since Lee walked right behind him, he did his best to take the pain in a manly, stoic silence, but he accidently let one ouchie slip. Or maybe two. Possibly three. But no more than that.

"Wow, your feet are really soft," Lee said.

"Hard as iron," Grant retorted.

"If iron were made of butterfly wings and puppy fluff."

Still grumbling at Lee's playful ribbing, Grant knelt beside the overturned carriage, inspecting it for any sign of tampering. Lee had said what happened to them wasn't an accident, but, so far, Grant wasn't finding any sign of foul play. Of course it didn't help that Lee hovered nearby, leaning over his shoulder to eye his progress and make little grunts that sounded sexual to Grant's ear. At least, he could visualize Lee's face pressed against his cheek, leaning forward as Grant rocked inside him. Was he an earlobe nibbler? With fangs like that, Grant assumed so.

"Mr. Noodle says hello." The fingers of Lee's shadow wiggled.

Grant fell onto his butt, which only offered a better view of his partial erection to the snickering Lee. Several rocks embedded themselves in his asscheeks, and he was sure at least one found the bullseye. This time, there'd be no denying his sexual attraction to Lee. Grant prepared himself for an endless string of apologies, one of which he hoped would convince his friend of so many years to forgive his slipup.

"Lee, I'm so sorry. I know how you—"

"Come on now, save it. One handsome little human in trouble, with a horse missing no less, and you're foaming at the mouth. Although I am happy to finally see you rise to the occasion. But, please, dear heart, do not fall in love with this guy."

Grant blinked. Somehow, Lee had missed the connection. "Oh, right. No falling in love with...with..." Shit what was his name? Grant risked peeking at the driver's nametag. "With Fredrick. Got it. Good advice."

In a guttural voice oddly out of character, Lee added, "Now focus. Like I said, this wasn't an accident. Notice the clawmarks near the wheel, detective."

Collecting as much of his scattered dignity as possible with rocks in his ass and his dick in the air, Grant got to his knees and studied the clawmarks Lee jabbed with his fingers.

"These look like—"

"Vampire claws. I *know*."

"Anyone here mad at you, other than Brian?"

Lee balked. "Why does it have to be me? You're the guy with the limp dick."

"Harsh."

"Well, it's true. Any of your failed one-night stands might be eager to send you a message about follow through."

Grant playfully slapped Lee on the shoulder. "Vampires really are bitches."

"True fact."

Splinters stuck out of the deep grooves cut into the wood; Grant pricked his finger on one as he ran it along the surface. He hid a wince and spit it out after he bit it from his flesh.

The latent anger Grant sensed with his heightened animal intuitions radiated from the gouge marks. Grant pressed his nose against them and inhaled, hoping to catch a whiff of the same mysterious vampire who stole his rabbit. He could open an investigation and not feel like a total fool—attempted murder was far less embarrassing than a stolen bunny.

Triumphant, Grant said, "Yes!"

"What is it?" Lee asked.

"Cologne and sunblock. Faint, but here. It's the same guy who took my damn rabbit."

Lee smacked his lips together. "Really?"

"Yes, really. I want to nail this asshole."

"Something tells me that if you'd nailed his asshole, we wouldn't be having these problems."

Grant struggled to come up with a suitably sharp retort, one that would impress the immortally unimpressed Lee, but he'd run out of steam. Not knowing what else to do, he made a show of reexamining the crime scene. The precise cuts on the horse's halter caught his eye. Earlier, Grant thought it odd when the horse immediately got away. He'd expected to hold the crying Lee, who was an animal lover, while he wept. Instead, the tethers had broken and Ned got away.

"What are you thinking?" Lee asked.

"This feels premeditated. But how would the vamp who did this know we were going to take a carriage ride?"

"Good question."

"Hm."

Lee's eyes narrowed on Grant's face. Grant struggled to interpret the sudden hostility that sparked between them, like a flame infused with oxygen. It was the type of anger that, if he blew on it, would burst into a dangerous, uncontained inferno. What did it mean, and where did it come from? They'd had a pleasant enough afternoon despite the near-death hiccup. Lee might have been slightly frustrated by Grant's inability to get with someone—Grant was being a bit of a wet blanket, he'd admit—but that wasn't something Lee had ever been angry about before.

"Lee—"

"Guys?" Fredrick called, interrupting him.

"Yes, Fredrick," Lee and Grant said together, sounding equally frustrated.

"The horse..."

Lee clapped his hands together. "Well, tenderfoot, you get back to the hotel and put on some clothes. Let Fred and I search for Ned."

Fredrick limped over to them, looking like he'd been put through a hell of a wringer. Dark circles drooped under his eyes, and he teetered as he staggered forward. Grant rushed forward and swept him in his arms before he fell. Cradling Fredrick close to his chest, he turned to Lee. "Okay, here's the plan. I'm going to get Fredrick here to a doctor. I'll get some clothes when that's done, and then you and I will grab a bite to eat. Afterward, let's put our heads together. Maybe we can crack this case."

"Sounds good," Lee said.

The sharp edge Lee carved on the two words increased the mystery surrounding his odd mood shifts. He'd been acting strangely the entire time—sullen, withdrawn, and seemingly fishing for something—but Grant couldn't put his finger on any cause other than Brian's unwelcome presence.

Earlier, he'd sensed latent hostile energy from the deep gouge marks on the carriage's side. He swore he sensed the same anger radiating from Lee, who followed them from a distance.

Chapter Seventeen

Everyone's eyes followed Grant's progress as he hauled Fredrick through the lobby. A few covered their mouths and snickered while others outright laughed at the spectacle of a naked shifter hauling around a human, who'd fainted in his arms. One or two followed along after Grant, examining his butt while they made appreciative wolf whistles.

"You have quite a following," Lee bit out. "Perhaps you'll escape the shadow of Limp Noodle yet. Not that it casts one, you haven't gotten *that* far."

"How about wererabbit? Will I escape that?"

Lee snorted. "Do you know where your rabbit is yet?"

"No." But now he had a hunch.

"Then no."

The hipster vampire with the stomach tattoo, who Grant decided to simply call Tattoo, stepped in front of them. He wiggled his eyebrows suggestively. "Seems you three have had a lot of fun without us. Maybe the human had too much, hmm?" To Lee, he said, "Did you drain him?"

"There was an accident," Grant said. "Our carriage wrecked. He passed out."

"Yes, our carriage driver is artfully dramatic," Lee drawled. "Our little extra."

Fredrick picked that moment to take a deep sigh and press his face against Grant's chest. His eyelids fluttered as his hand trailed up Grant's pecs, lingering on a pert nipple. The light touch startled Grant; he hopped in place, his feet, slick with sweat, squeaked on the marble floor. The jolt shook Fredrick awake. The young man opened his eyes. In a sleepy voice, he drawled, "What...what happened?"

Lee, fangs out like a spitting cobra, grunted.

Grant responded, "The carriage tipped over. Remember? We're back in the hotel. You're safe."

"Yes. Thank you so much. Can you take me to my room?"

Lee's lips pinched together and his cheeks puffed out until he resembled the screamer in the Van Gogh painting—pale wan cheeks, blurry features, and a fountain of angst erupting for eternity. When he ripped the hood off his head, his mane of chestnut hair frizzed out along his high cheekbones, which were blushed scarlet. He looked about ready to burst into a marathon of words, but, if that had been his intent, he must have thought better of it. He stayed quiet while his eyes—the colorful flames dancing—did the talking. He was pissed about something. That much was obvious.

God, why did his anger excite Grant so much? He wanted to lick those flames, knowing full well fire did all the burning. Never the other way around.

"Hello again, Mr. Noodle," Lee bit out. "I'll leave you and Fredrick to it. I'm going to go back out to find Ned."

"Wait for me. Let's get a bite to eat first," Grant called after him, but Lee only raised his hand and waved in response.

With a smirk playing at his lips, Tattoo watched the exchange from a distance. Occasionally, he let out an *aha* as though he'd made a breakthrough on an especially difficult scientific endeavor. There was something academic about his posture, his tilted head resting against a curled fist, Grant found unsettling. He had nothing against intellectuals. But he didn't care much for being studied.

"Can I help you?" Grant asked him.

Tattoo, holding his knuckle against his full bottom lip, clucked his tongue. "Not at all. This was... informative."

The lobby erupted in a new round of snickers that Grant had to climb two flights of stairs to escape. By the fifth floor, something dreadful occurred to him. "Uh, where is your room?"

Fredrick chuckled. "Basement. I'm staff, remember?"

"Of course. You have a room number down there?"

"B55."

After taking a deep breath, Grant ambled back down the stairs, hoping that a steady, light pace might keep him hidden and that he'd be able to book it down the hall without anyone noticing. Each time his dick hit his thighs, he swore it clapped like thunder. That was probably an overly flattering comparison, but the vampires in the lobby heard him coming, nonetheless. By the time he started his descent to the first floor, there was a gaggle of them in the lobby, whooping and jumping.

"Yes, yes," Grant said, pushing his way through the crowd. "I'm a mess. I know. Thank you."

A few patted him on the back as he made the journey from the stairs to the elevator. One of the bolder ones, Grant didn't know who, gave his butt a good slap, and someone shouted, "That's the spirit. Plow him like he's snow in July."

Fredrick's arms, which were looped around Grant's neck, tightened as the elevator jolted to action. He pressed his face against the slope of Grant's neck. In a breathy whisper, he said, "Sorry for being such a pain."

"Hey, no problem."

"You're so wonderful," Fredrick added. "My own personal hero."

"Don't mention it. Do you have your key?"

After Fredrick nodded, Grant set him on his feet, cupping his elbow to steady him in case he wobbled. As patiently as he could, Grant waited while the young man fished around in his pockets for his hotel key. In the meantime, he thought about Lee's strange moods and the odd anger he sensed from both the deep gouges in the carriage and his friend's demeanor.

Lee had the means and the opportunity to pull off the carriage stunt, but Grant couldn't fathom his friend having a motive, especially when either of them could have been seriously hurt.

"Are you...are you coming?" Fredrick asked.

"I've been asked that question a lot lately. You may have heard," Grant said, giving him a lopsided smile.

Fredrick blushed and nodded. "There have been rumors about your, uh, noodle." Grant's face must have betrayed some of his anxiety. Fredrick grabbed hold of Grant's bicep. Squeezing, he said, "But I like it! And it's more of a python, if you ask me."

That comparison seemed apt. Grant's dick was certainly choking the life out of him each time it popped up to say hello. But Grant didn't know what to say to the strange compliment or to Fredrick's overt attempt to hook up with him. He wanted to say no, but each time he nearly did, Fredrick's expression, hopeful and shy, begged for a yes. And, well, he hadn't run away when Grant transformed. There was that.

There was one other thing going for him. Fredrick didn't look like Lee—at all. His face was too round, too soft, too open and honest. No mischief lurked in the twitching corners of his mouth; his eyes were void of dark sarcasm. So far, he hadn't demonstrated a tendency for whimsical wordplay. Plus, he was far warmer than their initial meeting, where he'd read from a prepared script, suggested.

Grant said, "Okay, but you have to do me a small favor."

"What's that?"

"Say, 'Come here, fella' and give your knee a pat."

Laughing, Fredrick bent down and patted his knee. Whistling, he said, "Come on, fella."

Merriment made Fredrick's hazel eyes come to life, momentarily giving him a small fraction of Lee's allure, enough to get the noodle working.

Chapter Eighteen

Heart, if it's not too much to ask, can you direct some blood toward my head? At least route it away from my dick.

The plea, growing familiar to Grant each passing moment, came to mind when he met with Lee again. Although he'd told himself a satisfying romp with Fredrick would cure his occasional boner slipups, the opposite proved true. The moment he surged inside Fredrick, he only thought about how the young driver wasn't Lee and no one else ever would be. Then, when Lee opened the door to their shared room and sniffed him, the noodle acted up again. It was embarrassing. Him, a full-grown man and a werewolf to boot, acting like a horny high school jock.

"So, did you enjoy yourself with Fredrick?" Lee asked.

"Did you find Ned?" Grant countered.

"No, I didn't."

The sadness in Lee's voice tugged at his heart. "Let's go get that horse, then. Come on."

Lee brightened. "You think you can track him?"

"Yes. I have a very sensitive nose."

The full-beam smile Lee gave him afterward made a long evening of slogging through the forest a win rather than a tedious chore. Joy shifted the color of Lee's eyes to a sort of emerald blue, a shade of water that promised to be warm but deep.

"Let me get my hoodie!"

Lee rarely exclaimed about anything, so Grant grinned at his raw enthusiasm, which didn't subside when the minutes began to rack up and Lee didn't reappear.

Earlier, Grant reminded Lee of his keen sense of smell, to push a confession. After a day of searching, he had a pretty good idea of who may have spirited off Lucky, the missing bunny. He didn't want to make accusations until he was sure, but all signs pointed to his animal-loving friend, whose clothes still smelled a bit too much like Lucky for Grant to dismiss the theory. Originally, he'd ruled out Lee as a suspect because his scent would naturally be in their shared room.

But that would mean the bunny thief and the sunblock and cologne combo suspect were different vamps. Grant didn't like that one bit.

Lee drifted out of the bathroom to stand in front of the long mirror attached to the closet door. Studying his reflection, he swiped his hand across his brow, tucking in the loose strands of chestnut hair that dared to escape the confines of the hoodie.

"We only have a half hour of daylight left—max. So, I wouldn't spend too much time gussying up," Grant said, wondering whose eye his friend was trying to catch. He hadn't seen Lee with any other humans since the Unicorn, who Grant didn't think was really all that special. If you asked him. Which no one had.

"Well, one can never be too sure," Lee said. As if to drill home the point, he continued to pivot left and right, striking different poses in front of the mirror. "Yes, yes. Fabulous. Much sparkle. Well worth making Grant wait a few extra of his precious seconds."

"Okay, okay. Remember poor Ned who's probably out there galloping all alone, cold and afraid with wolves circling around him."

"Oh, dear heart, that is a cruel image."

Doing his best to imitate a horse, which no doubt made him look totally ridiculous, Grant clomped around the room and fake cried. "I'm Ned. Boo hoo. I died for Lee's mediocre fashion."

"Low blow."

"Come on. Let's get going. I want to find this thing before the restaurant closes."

"He's not a thing; he's a *he*," Lee grumbled, grabbing his keys while heading toward the door.

As they strolled down the hall, Grant discreetly sniffed Lee. Yeah, Lucky's dander clung to Lee's skin and clothes but no sunblock. Judging by the freshness of the odor and its location on his body, Lee'd been cuddling the damn rabbit somewhat recently. He hadn't even released the creature back out into the forest. Somewhere in the hotel, he'd stashed Grant's midnight snack. Had Lee also been responsible for the carriage wreck? Grant doubted it, but he couldn't deny the coincidences added up to a pretty strong question mark.

Grant coughed, clearing his throat.

"Something you want to say?"

"Remember how we said we'd never be those people who don't talk and cause drama by keeping secrets from each other?"

Lee shot him a sideways glance. "I seem to remember something along those lines. Have a confession you'd like to make? The booth is open."

"Do you want to tell me anything...?"

"No..."

"Come on, I know it was you."

"What was me?"

Tossing his hands in the air, Grant nearly shouted, "The rabbit! You've got Lucky!"

For a long while, Lee said nothing, but Grant swore he heard the gears turning in his friend's head while he thought of a suitable response. Finally, he echoed Grant's dramatic gesture. "And what if I do?"

"I was going to eat it."

"He's not an it! He's a he! And he's my precious little bunnywuvs."

"Bunnywuvs?"

"Don't sound so disgusted!"

Grant didn't think he could manage to fulfill the last request. Trying his best, he said, "Where is bunnywuvs now?"

"I'm not telling you, you big bad midnight snacker!"

Growling low in his throat—an irritated, not vicious noise, and Lee damn well knew the difference—Grant stalked down the hall and did his best not to breakdown and threaten the lives of every bunny from the East to West Coasts. Such posturing would only earn him a harsh reprimand from his sensitive friend, not the location of his prey. After a good period of sulking, he said, "I'm going to find Lucky."

"Nope."

"Yup, I will. Then, I'm going to eat him."

Lee gasped. "You would not! Not after we named him!"

"*You* named him."

"Yes, but he's our child. It was a joint venture."

There was nothing Grant could say about that, so he stuttered in indignation, throwing in a snort or two for good measure. To think that he, a majestic wolf, might foster a rodent was inconvincible. Grant, highlighting the point, stuck his fist against his palm. "Like hell that stinking tidbit is my family."

Lee whirled on him and stuck his finger right into Grant's chest. Using his vampire strength, he nudged Grant against a wall. "You're not getting Lucky! Find another defenseless creature, you heartless brute!"

"I'm going to eat the shit out of that rabbit!"

A door to another hotel room opened. A blurry-eyed vampire stepped out into the hall to glower at them. "Keep it down. Some of us are sleeping. And, for what it's worth, I agree with the werewolf: rabbits are for eating. Now shut the fuck up and go away."

Grant flipped his hands in the air. "Thanks, that's what I'm saying!"

Lee pointed at Grant, then at the blinking vampire. "You're both total assholes."

He nearly made it to the elevator before Grant caught up to him again. While he struggled to close the gap, he debated whether or not his reaction had been over the top. Stealing someone else's dinner, especially when that someone was your best friend, put Lee square in the at-fault box. Grant knew that for sure. But he'd maybe gone overboard and channeled his other frustrations.

"Lee...?"

Lee tapped his foot while they waited for the elevator, which was all the way down in the lobby.

"Don't freeze me out. I'm sorry. I won't eat the damn rabbit."

"Lucky."

"Yes, Lucky. I won't eat him. There, you happy?"

"More so."

Grant nudged him with his elbow. "What can I do to get you back to ecstatic? Imitate the horse again? I know you smiled at that. You couldn't hide it under the hoodie."

"No, I didn't."

Grant clomped around near the elevator. "I'm poor sad Ned, lost in the woods with only my hooves to keep me glued together."

"Groan, dear heart."

"Reject me, then. I'm used to hearing neigh."

The elevator doors slid open right as Grant let loose an actual neigh. The vampires on the other side of the door, every last one of them, raised their right eyebrow. When one of them said, "Looks like we've reached floor whackjob" the rest nodded.

Lee had always been right about one thing. Vampires were total bitches.

Chapter Nineteen

In the dim evening light, the floor of the forest was nothing but cast shadows from the overhanging trees. Light, what tiny amounts escaped from the filter of the thick evergreen canopy, illuminated the outlines of trees but little else. Despite the lack of sunlight, Lee kept his hoodie drawn over his head, hiding his features from Grant's view and keeping his thoughts to himself. For all of ten minutes, Grant attempted conversation, but Lee only offered monosyllable responses before drifting back off to a tense silence.

"You okay?" Grant asked for the fifth time.

"Yeah."

Vampires, as nocturnal creatures, had wonderful night vision. That's why Lee sliding his slender hand into Grant's larger paw confused Grant. Independent almost to a fault, Lee rarely let anyone help him. And now he was being led through the maze of overturned stumps, barely even noticing where his feet fell. Lee's hand, slick with sweat, added another puzzle to the mix. What on earth was he, a vampire, nervous about?

"Are you still mad about Lucky?" Grant guessed.

"No. I know you wouldn't eat him, fluff-a-luff-a-gus."

Grant's heart did a backflip when Lee said the cute nickname, but he forced himself to focus on the matter at hand. Some hidden problem ate at his friend's normally cheery mood, and he was going to uncover the reason after enough prying and nagging. "What's going on, then? Something's bothering you."

"You sound paranoid. Also, you promised no more questions."

"Lee, tell me—"

Suddenly, Lee stumbled on some underbrush, pitching forward with a startled yelp closely followed by a cussword. Grant shot forward to swoop him in his arms. The surge of heat between their bodies loosened his already tenuous hold on his wayward libido. Matters weren't helped when Lee twined his arms around his neck and cradled his head in the safe nook under Grant's chin.

"Lee."

"You're out of breath. I can't weigh that much."

"No." God, what was he going to say? That he longed to strip off their clothes and rut on the forest floor until both of them—panting, sweaty—howled and thrashed in the throes of pleasure that bordered on pain? Nope. He wasn't going to say *that*. "Uh, I think I picked up the scent of the horse."

An excited gasp escaped Lee's mouth. The hot air of his breath licked the hollow of Grant's throat, and he wished for Lee's tongue to graze the same tender spot— every bit as slow and warm. *Bad thoughts. Bad.*

"There, you okay?" Grant asked as he placed Lee on the ground. "No scuffs?"

Lee gave him a salute. "Scuff free, detective. Which direction is the horse?"

Oh, right, that's the lie he'd told to get himself out of accidentally revealing his desires and shattering Lee's fragile trust and then possibly losing his friendship for forever. No pressure. Grant made a show of sniffing the air, pivoting his body left, right, center until he actually— thankfully—did pick up on a faint earthy smell of manure.

"This way."

"Don't suppose you'd carry me there the way you did Fredrick?"

"Sure, climb on board."

Grant squatted so Lee could hop onto his back.

"No, I meant..."

"You meant what?"

"Never mind."

Lee jumped and wrapped his arms around Grant's neck. Digging his heels into Grant's ribs, he shouted, "Giddyup! Ya!"

To get through the ordeal of being a substitute horse, Grant's imagination slapped Lee in a pair of tight leather chaps and had him say the same thing while he rode Grant's dick. Bonus: Lee couldn't see his erect cock with his face mashed against Grant's neck.

"What, no more horse sounds?" Lee griped.

Love was a bigger bitch than vampires and both rode him equally hard this entire trip. Grant whinnied.

"Fantastic," Lee purred into Grant's ear. "You're so good to me."

"Glad to amuse, as always."

"Are you still on the trail of our missing horse?"

"Yeah."

Thankfully, he heard the damn creature now, so he stopped sniffing the air to trace the stench of its manure. Instead, he depended on his keen ears and listened to Ned drag the remains of his harness through the underbrush. The metal elements rattled while the leather squeaked. Occasionally, he'd whinny, stomping his hooves on the ground like a toddler throwing a tantrum.

"He's pretty pissed off," Grant said. "Hope you can talk him down.'"

"Poor baby. He's had a hell of a night."

"Him and me both. One more hour of not eating, and I might gnaw my own arm off. You know low blood sugar makes me a fluff-a-*grump-a-lus*. After this, it's dinner time."

"Oh, get down off your cross."

Grant chuckled. "I thought you were going to say high horse."

Lee's heels dug into Grant's sides, tickling his ribs. "We've talked about this issue of yours...taking the low-hanging fruit."

The friendly quarrel would have to wait. Up ahead in a clearing, Ned snapped at the end of his tether, which had wrapped itself around stumps and dangling branches. There was enough slack left in the reins to allow Ned to move his head but little wiggle room otherwise. Overturned dirt and pyramid-shaped piles of manure littered the area around his feet and he continued to dig, dotting the ground with hoofprint gouges.

Like most animals, Ned sensed neither Grant nor Lee were human. Grant assumed the horse had been trained around supernatural creatures, given his comfort level during the carriage ride, but maybe he'd overestimated how much exposure Ned had. As they approached, the horse rolled his eyes and stomped. His head whipped backward, and he let loose a loud and high whinny, growing more agitated as they neared his flank.

Shushing the spooked beast, Lee held out his hand and rested it against Ned's nose. He rubbed the long snout while whispering comforting words in the animal's hooked ear. A slow smile spread across his face when the horse nuzzled him. Ned's soft lips nibbled Lee's fingers, and he whinnied again, this time in contentment.

"I think he likes me!" Lee beamed.

"Yeah, animals love you."

While Lee soothed the beast, Grant studied the remains of the harness and reins that had attached the animal to the carriage. Deep claw marks scarred the straps, leaving lighter stripes in the dark leather. Like before, Grant's supernatural senses detected smoldering anger and sharp bitterness. He grabbed the straps and sniffed, hoping to get a solid lead, but he only uncovered the same twisted odors of sunblock and cheap grocery store cologne from before. Only, it was overwhelmingly strong. Whoever did this had already found Ned.

"What is it?" Lee asked, bending down next to him.

"We might have a problem."

"More trouble in paradise?"

"Yeah. Our culprit is masking their scent with products. You were right when you said this is premeditated, and whoever's doing it is making it difficult to track them."

"Fantastic. What are we going to do?"

Grant shrugged. "Go back to the hotel and get Ned back to his stall, I guess. Not much else we can do right now."

Together, they untangled the horse and removed the rest of the harness, leaving only the reins. On a whim, Grant lifted Lee up to the horse's bare back, chuckling when his friend gasped in surprise but then belted out a delighted whoop. In his excitement, Lee's undead flesh took on a hint of rose and his eyes—oh those lovely eyes— danced to the beat of Grant's heart.

Lee looked down with all the haughty authority of an aristocrat about ready to embark on a foxhunt. "Am I amazing? Say yes."

"Yes," Grant whispered. He tried to say the word again, this time with more macho authority, but he only managed a more breathless version of the same admission.

Lee tilted his head. His eyes darkened and widened at the same time, hinting that maybe he wrestled with the same impulses Grant had struggled to control their entire trip. Lips parted, he rested his gaze on the swell of Grant's neck and drained his will as surely as if he'd sipped the last drop of his blood.

"Grant?"

"Yes?"

He licked his lips and flushed. The stain of red on his pale skin cut a path across his sharp cheekbones, appearing, for a moment, cosmetic rather than natural. "You're, uh, you're..."

"I'm..."

A little bit too loudly, Lee said, "Not pulling the horse forward. Giddyup."

An agitated groan almost broke free from Grant's mouth, but he shoved it back deep down where it couldn't cause trouble. Also, a tad too loud, he said, "Sorry, I got lost in my thoughts. Trying to puzzle together the mystery of our carriage saboteur."

"Always on duty."

"Right."

While he struggled to control his errant thoughts, Grant did actually consider the strange series of events that had plagued their short but seemingly cursed vacation. The miscreant, whoever it was, had thought about how to mask their trail. These weren't impulsive acts but well-thought-out little jabs of mischief—petty and almost nonsensical. Also, mostly harmless. And the horse. The culprit made sure it was spared.

"Are you mad at me about something? Is that why you've been so moody?"

"I'm a vampire. Being moody is my dark calling."

"Don't deflect. You know what I mean."

Lee frowned. "No, not quite. Spit out what you're thinking."

Taking a deep breath, Grant said, "Did you have anything to do with the carriage?"

Chapter Twenty

The playful fire in Lee's eyes snuffed out to be replaced by an inferno of green and brown. Unholy light flickered behind the thin human curtain he'd drawn over his supernatural alter ego. "Excuse me?"

Well, he couldn't take it back. Sighing, Grant said, "You heard me. Did you have anything to do with the carriage?"

Sputtering like a riled cat that'd been thrown in a tub of cold water, Lee jumped down off the horse and landed without even a whisper of fabric or a light thud of footfall. Lithe and agile in his fury, he stalked forward and jabbed his index finger against Grant's chest. He was, however, less verbally graceful when provoked. "You're a total asshole."

"What?"

"You heard me."

Ned, as if pantomiming Lee's indignation, whinnied and flicked his head. The tangled strands of his mane flopped side to side.

Grant, who wasn't sure if he was talking to the horse or Lee, said, "It's a fair question."

"Like hell it is."

"Look, you've been acting weird this entire trip— skulking about in a doom cloud one second and then fawning over pretty boys the next. And then—"

Lee clenched his fists at his side. After a stomp of his foot, he said, "Fawning over pretty boys was the reason we came here, you big dope!"

"Sure, but—"

"But what!" Before Grant responded, Lee got in his face to shout, "And what's my motive? Why would I risk getting singed?"

That's exactly what Grant had been trying to figure out, and he didn't have an answer. Yet. Meanwhile, he'd have to settle for making shit up, because he damn well wasn't going to concede the argument to Lee, the demon himself who tormented the best of angels. "Spite!"

"Spite?"

"Yes! Spite!"

"You think I'd risk your life for *spite*?"

At that moment, Ned interjected with a high, distinctly annoyed-sounding whinny, which acted as a sort of a bell between rounds. Grant—his massive round chest heaving in and out—and Lee—fangs erect on the curve of his lip—split to their separate corners to size each other up.

From experience, Grant knew Lee's stamina and lust for the fight wouldn't wane no matter the occasion. A comet could crash down between them in this precise moment and Lee would sidestep it on his way to verbally backhand Grant for his temerity. If such endurance translated to a more carnal passion, Grant might be ecstatic to find himself in this situation. As it was, he was helpless in the face of Lee's staying power. This would have to be a KO.

Snapping his fingers, Grant spat out a sudden revelation. "I got it! To cover up taking the rabbit!"

"What?"

"That's why you sabotaged the carriage ride. To hide your guilt over Lucky!"

Lee's raised eyebrow was like cocking a gun. Steeling himself to dodge whatever bullet came from Lee's mouth chamber, Grant crouched down and focused his eyes, which he was sure glowed an intense yellow, on Lee's next move.

After circling Grant twice, he said, "Here's the scoop: you're a shit detective. Perhaps you should cultivate other talents, like deductive logic and rely less on your supernatural advantages and you'd be less of a lummox."

Honestly, *yes*, he'd been a shit detective this whole trip, but it wasn't his fault his senses muddled around Lee. Grant blamed his less than stellar performance across all categories on the brief moment of hope he'd known when Lee revealed he'd purposefully booked a single room.

Of course he couldn't admit Lee had a point.

A whole list of solid defenses, also intelligent ones, scrolled through Grant's mind. He flicked past all those acceptable songs, tried-and-true chestnuts, and pressed the play button on the one most likely to make an ass of him. "I changed my mind! I'm having rabbit stew! That's right. You want me to get lucky? Well, I will!"

"If you intend to get Lucky the rabbit the way you went about simply getting lucky, I'm not worried."

"What's that supposed to mean?"

Lee flipped his hands in the air. "Go on, get Lucky! If you can."

Grant growled. The vibrations rumbled in his chest cavity. "I'm going to eat that fucking rabbit, just you wait!"

Lee grabbed hold of Ned's reins and glared down the length of his aquiline nose. The haughty tilt to his chin spelled out the fact that their quarrel had reached its natural conclusion, with Lee the victor and Grant the conquered. Then, that had been the state of affairs before the whole thing started, and Grant supposed that was the crux of the problem.

Lee clicked his tongue to indicate Ned should follow. On cue, the horse neighed and fell in line behind the vampire, not even allotting a second glance for the downtrodden Grant as the two of them exited, stage left.

Alone with his blood pounding in his ears—for once, in his head instead of his cock—Grant replayed the entire scene as he took a different route back to the hotel. How had he so colossally bumbled the spat? At one point, he'd rounded and figuratively punched himself in the face a few times. Though, it served him right to bring the accusation without evidence.

"Good going," he chided, "you total idiot."

The steps to the grand hotel seemed steeper as he forced his stiff legs to lift and fall through the motions of going up. In protest, his right calf muscle seized in a tight knot he had to bend and massage out before he continued. As he lifted his head, a flurry of fresh snow, which instantly became water once it hit his hot skin, blew back in his face. The sudden frigid gust stole the moisture from his throat, and he let out a dry, hacking cough.

The hotel wasn't far away, but Grant had to give himself a long pep talk before he finally reached the last step.

The moment the door attendants stepped aside to usher him in, a group of vampires—each holding a goblet of blood—raised their fine crystal glasses in a mock toast. News traveled fast. Or they were just always catty. Grant was starting to think the latter.

Tattoo, the most persistent would-be lover Grant had ever known, drifted toward him. Dabs of blood wet his bottom lip. His pink tongue darted out and slid across the slick surface of his mouth to mop the spillage. In his fluting, pleasant voice, he said, "We weren't sure you'd come back."

"My stuff is in my room," Grant responded, casually throwing his hands in the air. "No choice."

The vampires tittered. Tattoo swirled the blood around in his goblet and ran his finger under the curve of Grant's jaw. Leaning in, he whispered, "Words are travelers too. And yours lifted thumbs for many ears tonight."

The thought that all the vampires of Lee's clan had overheard the entire altercation in the woods brought an angry flush to Grant's face. Didn't they have any sense of decorum?

Grant managed a pinched smile, a skill he'd mastered after many years of dealing with the public. "You all have a wonderful night."

Lee chose that moment to enter the room. Somehow, despite the long day and trying evening, he managed to illuminate the surroundings with his strange, dignified beauty. Wild and windblown, the long locks of his chestnut hair fluttered against the sides of his sharp cheekbones, which still had a hue of pink after their fight. All the colors of his iris tangled in a cacophony of light. And his lips, oh those deadly lips, curled upward in his ever-so-mischievous smile.

Grant wanted to kiss him. Or run away.

When nothing happened after their eyes met, Grant breathed a sigh of relief and assumed they'd sleep off their differences and meet as friends again in the morning light.

Being in the same room would make everyday living awkward until they mended fences, but they'd endured worse than agitated teeth brushing. He lifted his hand in a sheepish wave, but Lee's eyes narrowed at the half-apologetic gesture, and he pinched his lips together as though he'd been flipped the bird.

"Enjoying the party?" Lee asked.

"About to retire for the night, actually."

"Not going to eat first?"

Grant tried to inject humor into his tone when he said, "Holding out for rabbit. Remember?"

Lee's nostrils flared. For an amount of time so minuscule Grant only barely noticed, Lee's eyes widened and turned black, as cold as space. He had only seen Lee in the same state once before: the night he described Brian's ultimatum to abandon the vampire lifestyle and join him in mortality. Betrayal had been the word on his lips. Was it there now?

Afraid Lee might have taken his light jest as a serious threat, which wasn't a stretch, considering they'd recently argued, Grant started his apology, but he didn't get far into it before Lee floated toward him. Curling his lip in a snarl, his breath hot on Grant's face, he said, "Not everything in this world is meant to be devoured. Something you can't understand as a dumb monster."

Grant staggered backward. Inside his chest, his wounded heart thudded as though the damn thing were running up a staircase away from the altercation.

"Grant..."

Tears welled in the corners of Lee's eyes as his chin trembled. He opened his mouth as if to say something, and Grant would have settled for anything, but instead of offering an apology, Lee set his face in a stern glower, which he couldn't quite hold. Despite his best efforts to remain stoic, fat tears spilled over his cheeks.

"Excuse me," Grant said. There wasn't much else he could say with his throat constricting, so he turned and left with as much dignity as he could muster with vampires snickering behind him. Lee called his name again, but Grant's mind focused on one word: monster.

Chapter Twenty-One

Happily, not a single soul joined him in the elevator. Once the doors shut, he stood alone with his back pressed against the mirrors lined along the wall, probably leaving stubborn smudges for the night janitor to clean. Grant tried not to care about making the vampire's job harder than it ought to be, but—damn it—he'd been raised to consider the feelings of others. He'd inherited his father's blue eyes, his father's dark hair, his father's massive bulk and tendency to slouch, but he had his mother's heart, romantic and gentle. It wasn't the heart of a dumb beast, an animal, a monster.

He didn't mean it, Grant told himself. Despite his own reassurances, tears pricked behind his eyelashes. Grant wiped them away with the back of his hand and added, *He's upset about something else. That's all*. Also, Grant knew he'd been a total ass to accuse Lee without any evidence, but he wasn't ready to admit it out loud.

With a tired sigh, he pushed away from the glass and turned to study the extent of the mess. Chuckling a bit, he studied the two half-moon imprints his butt left behind. It was appropriate—he'd definitely been showing his ass in more than one way and seemed destined to always have it hanging out in the wind.

Unfortunately, he didn't have anything handy to wipe off the smudges. Wet from the snow, his sleeves would likely smear across the glass. He'd have to return to clean the mess. That was all there was to it.

The bell dinged and the doors slid open. The vampire on the other side startled, rocking backward on his heels when he saw Grant. Once he realized who it was, he smirked before sliding past him into the elevator. Almost as cheekily, he slapped his hand on the buttons and swiped downward, lighting up each floor. "Bye," he said, giving Grant a chipper wave.

Shaking his head, Grant pondered the strange nature of vampires. He could live to be a million, and he still wouldn't understand their behavior. But wasn't that what he loved most about his friend? Unpredictable, unexplainable, Lee jumped out of every box Grant had ever tried to put him in, all while maintaining his strange charm that allowed for innumerable transgressions.

Grant paused in the hallway. The concocted scent of the mischief-maker he'd been trailing—the overwhelming cheap cologne and sunblock mixture—hovered in the air, easily detectable and almost fresh. Nose in the air, Grant followed the zigzagging path of the stench until he butted against the door to the room he shared with Lee.

This would make the second time the reeking vampire broke into their room.

Mindful of the security camera, and how strange he must appear, Grant pressed his nose against the paper-thin gaps between door and wall and inhaled. Behind the thick curtain of the mischief-maker's putrid camouflage, Grant's nose detected a peep of what might perhaps be his true scent: an understated mixture of salt and pine.

The strange anger he'd detected at the carriage and on the horse's tattered leather straps simmered in the air, leaving behind a meager but noticeable emotional residue. Sensing danger, Grant's inner animal tilted its ears forward and listened for the perpetrator. Hearing nothing, he slid in his key.

As he entered the room, Grant scanned each nook and cranny just in case the vamp had hidden. During his search, Grant cataloged changes in the environment, noting the toiletries on their bathroom counter had been shoved to one side and their towels thrown on the floor. Grant bent and sniffed each individual item, but for his efforts he only got trace amounts of salt and pine and a heavy dose of cologne and sunblock. The unpleasant goulash of odors induced a fit of sneezing.

When Grant studied his reflection in the mirror, he noted a slew of red veins threading through the whites of his eyes. Bending over the sink, he flung water into his face, hoping to clear his body's nasty reaction to the mischief-maker's rather potent funk.

"Jesus," Grant muttered to himself when his ablutions made little difference.

He toweled off his face using a washcloth he'd picked up from the floor. It smelled the best out of all of them, so it would have to do until he mustered the hutzpah to wander back to the lobby and request more towels from whatever mocking vampire staffed the front desk. In the meantime, he'd pull a fresh shirt from his bag and then go attend to the embarrassing smudge on the glass mirrors in the elevator.

At least that was the plan.

The absence of another odor struck him full force as he entered the sleeping area of the hotel room. Lee's scent, subtle and calming like a fresh rain tinged with lemon soap, had faded from the room, leaving behind the chemicals used to clean the sheets and Grant's own musk. And Lee's bags were missing.

He'd left a note on the bed: *Dear heart, masturbation is a lot like the state of nature: poor, nasty, brutish, and short. Enjoy both. Your next cheesecake is on me.*

On the other side, he'd attached twenty dollars.

Grant growled.

The logical part of his brain, the hemisphere that realized his friend hadn't reeked of sunblock, screamed Lee was unlikely to be the culprit and his friend's only sin was being a dick. The emotional side of his brain hit a big red button that said, *Go on, get Lucky.* As in, time to slather some butter on bread to make himself a bunny sandwich.

Grant dressed in a fresh pair of pants and shirt. A contentious citizen first and a rabbit killer second, he grabbed enough tissues from the hotel's complimentary stash to clean the glass and stuffed them in his pockets.

Grant strolled down the hall with purpose. Even the rude vampires he encountered along the way didn't deter him or shake his resolve. This time, the wolf whistles brought out the wolf. Showing his teeth in a feral grin, he stared them down until they flattened themselves against the wall and squeaked by. He took some pleasure in hearing them scramble away, their dainty vampire feet pattering on the dense carpet.

Happy to have his confidence back, Grant lifted his head high and came as close to strutting as dignity allowed. He didn't want to go too overboard. After all, he wasn't off to fight a battle for the heart and soul of man or even to take down the mischief-maker plaguing his vacation time. Nothing so useful or worthy of swagger. But, if anyone asked the reason for his sudden mood boost, he'd tell a nice lie along those lines.

He was going to do it. He was going to eat that damn rabbit.

Chapter Twenty-Two

Okay, Grant wasn't going to eat the rabbit. Yes, he was. No he wasn't. *Yes*, he was.

Massive flakes of snow fluttered to the ground, indicating the temperature hadn't plummeted enough to sap all the moisture from the air. Grant stood in front of the window, close enough that his breath left pulsing circles of condensation, and pondered his strategy. Finding the rabbit would be child's play. Getting it away from Lee, well, that would require some finesse. He had to solve the puzzle before playing the game.

"Hey, again."

This time he'd kept himself acutely aware of the environment, so Tattoo hadn't really snuck up on him. Now that his thoughts of romance had dissipated, his blood helpfully flowed to his brain. He'd hoped the persistent vamp would be discouraged by his lack of attention and go away. No such luck, apparently. He came from behind and placed an overly familiar hand on Grant's shoulder, to which he gave a light squeeze.

"Hey," Grant said.

"You're so strong," Tattoo said. "It's a shame to keep seeing you all alone when we could be having so much fun."

Grant shrugged to remove the vamp's hand, but he only chuckled lightly and tightened his grip until the light pressure became a sharp pinch. Grant forced a calm, stoic frame of mind as the vamp's nails dug into the skin along his collarbone. Droplets of blood ran down his chest, getting as far as his pecs before it dried. Later, flakes would peel off like dead skin; the rest would wash off easily enough, and his black T-shirt wouldn't show the stain. And that's what Grant thought about to keep from screaming.

Tattoo whistled. "I've heard about you, by the way. Running away from the Big Bad Wolf stories back home?"

Denying the truth of it would be nonsensical. "How did you read about that here? There's no internet."

"I didn't *read* about it. It's called a land line. Am I the only one old enough to remember what that is?"

Grant's heart opened the floodgates and sent a wave of red blood to stain his cheeks a hot crimson. Outdated technology, which brought the story to his vampire co-vacationers just as well as a Twitter feed or Instagram post, transported his troubles from home to here. He'd been foolish to think he could run from his woes. The modern world didn't allow it.

Later, Grant would hate himself for asking, but he had to know the answer. "And what's David saying?"

"That you're brutish company, a dumb animal focused on things like sex and hunting. Let me just say I wish it were true."

"Yes, I get the impression you'd like me to be more amenable." Dreading the answer, especially if David had accused him of worse, he asked, "Anything else?"

"No, just a lot about you being a big, dumb monster with no sense of class or style."

Oddly, Grant's heart only squeezed painfully when he pictured the words coming from Lee's mouth, not David's. His ex, a ghost haunting his past life, already fit neatly into the folder holding all the rest of his failed romances—men who'd reminded him of Lee but never came close to being the real thing. Miserable, realizing he'd been an ass to his past lovers, including David, Grant began to unravel the pattern of his behavior.

Grant realized Tattoo still had his claws digging into his shoulder when he backed up, forcing the nails deeper into his flesh. A whole new wash of blood rolled down his chest; this time reaching the waistband of his dark jeans.

Tattoo whistled again. "Wow, you can take a lot. Again, we can have *so much* fun."

Grant thought it was cute when Lee stressed his words, especially when he crinkled his nose like some undead grandma. When this vamp did it, Grant repressed a tired sigh and an accompanying eye roll. "No, thank you. I've found my own amusements."

Tattoo chuckled. "You never gave me even a slight chance to change your mind."

That was true. Since the first day they met, Grant had read something in Tattoo he didn't quite trust. There was no accounting for the odd sensation, other than instinct, a feeling of persistent unease. But Tattoo didn't reek of sunblock, cheap cologne, or salt and pine, so there was no reason to suspect him of anything beyond being an annoying creeper and a pain fetishist.

"There's no changing it. I'm not into you, and I won't be no matter how often you ask."

Drawing back, Tattoo placed his hand on his chest to simulate hurt, but the corners of his mouth twisting upward and the sharp glint in his predatory eyes undercut the illusion. "My goodness, you are a prickly pear."

"Guess so. Please excuse me."

"You'll regret not taking advantage of my offer!"

He was already halfway back down the hall. The shouted warning heaped on Grant's already full plate of things he might have to deal with later. Worse, the unwelcome conversation distracted him from the task at hand, the whole business about killing and eating Lucky, and made him doubt the wisdom of the scheme in the first place.

Grant zipped inside one of the elevators, already almost packed to capacity, before it closed. He remained standing face forward instead of turning around to stand shoulder to shoulder with his fellow passengers. A few coughed into their hands to hide their slight smiles. Their amusement with his odd behavior at least provided them with some story fodder.

Besides, he had to endure some contact if he was still going to find and eat Lucky.

Or maybe you should sit down with Lee and talk about your feelings instead, his reflection said on behalf of his heart.

Shut up, reflection, he said back.

"Sorry," he told the crowd. "Can't spin around very easily without pushing someone. I thought this would be better, even if you have to look at my ugly mug."

"No problem," the nearest vampire said. "Though I do miss the view of your ass."

A round of good-natured chuckles brought smiles to the faces in front of him, making them appear less cruel than their previous encounters suggested. Perhaps they'd been trying to get him to warm to them all along. Vampires, in general, were a lot less uptight and more carefree than werewolves, Grant found.

Matching the vamp's teasing tone, Grant said, "Well, we still have four more days. My past history says you'll be seeing my ass again. I seem to be a repeat offender."

The quip earned him another round of smiles and appreciative laughs. One offered a high five. Grant obliged.

"So, are you going to talk to him?" the high five vampire asked.

"Who?"

As if plugged into the same hive mind, they turned to the nearest vampire and shared a disbelieving shrug and knowing look. "Your little bunny snatcher," a female vamp eventually said, flicking her wrist as if she were flipping ash away from a lit cigarette. "But we're calling him the Noodle Whisperer."

Goddamn, vampires were really into nicknames.

The mirror in the back of the elevator showed his face, pinched and wan from hunger and stress, as it turned red. Despite his previous statement, he tried to turn around in the cramped elevator, but he couldn't move an inch without stepping on someone's foot or bumping his hip.

"Oh, don't hide your face. We love how big and awkward you are," a vamp near the back said. "Also, a little birdy told me your missing snack might be in a woodshed near the outdoor fire pits."

"Now the poor thing will get goobled for sure," another vampire quipped.

"I guess I like playing cupid." To Grant he said, "You're not actually going to eat the poor fluffball, are you?"

"No, no," Grant denied. "I'm just going to...uh..."

"Totally eat him..." another vamp supplied.

Grant cocked a mischievous eyebrow. "Every last scrap."

But he wasn't, not really.

Chapter Twenty-Three

The snow, now nearly a foot deep, worked its way through the top cracks of his impractical sneakers he'd worn because his lust-driven prefrontal cortex refused to make sensible decisions. Water soaked through his thin socks to his feet within a matter of minutes. Large flakes fluttered across the sky, cutting diagonally right in his face. No matter how he turned and twisted his body, the wind seemed to shift with him. Although the temperature wasn't as frigid as it had been previously, Grant seriously considered ripping up another outfit to transform to wolf. He *had* promised to show his butt again.

Traces of moonlight reflected off the glittering snow, illuminating the dark shadows of the trees towering above him. Structures, the various toolsheds and gardening stations, stood out in contrast, and Grant checked each one he came across, hoping to eventually hit pay dirt before he froze to death in his absurd quest.

Occasionally, whiffs of sunblock and cheap cologne traveled in his direction. Before Grant traced the scent's path, the wind tore it away, dispersing the trail of it through the air. Grant mentally shrugged. Let the mischief-maker confront him here. At least that would mask Grant's insanity in a convenient lie and he could tell anyone who asked that he'd come out here to find his tormentor rather than to chase after a bunny.

By now, he inwardly admitted he had no intention of eating Lucky. Rather, he thought he might find Lee and their two hearts, cornered by the storm, would find themselves needing the same thing.

"You're a total idiot," Grant said. But he kept walking forward.

Up ahead, unnatural light flickered through the air, dense with snowfall. Grant wrapped his arms around himself and plowed through the snow, leaving behind a long trail of sloppy footprints, until he reached the outside of a shed. The structure rattled each time the wind blew through the cracks in the wooden boards, where the light peeped through.

"Hello?" Grant said. He didn't want to accidently walk in on a couple in the middle of a sexual encounter. He didn't detect any of the telltale signs of hanky panky, but it was hard to smell anything with his nose half frozen, and they could be quiet lovers. "Hello? Anyone in there?"

When no one answered, Grant grabbed hold of the rope connected to a metal peg and pulled. The door slid open. Behind it, the rabbit that started it all scratched his long ear with his elongated back leg. Lee had dressed him in some type of sweater he must have made himself. At least, Grant hadn't seen any gift shops with cute animal costumes in the hotel.

When Lucky saw Grant, he spit out a string of poop.

"Sorry, Lucky," Grant said. "Didn't mean to scare you."

Apparently, Lucky wasn't quite buying it. His paws skidded on the wooden floor; his claws left behind tiny scratches, lighter on the dark and aging wood. In his rush to flee, he turned and bopped his head straight into a wall. Grant, glad Lee was nowhere nearby, allowed himself a dark chuckle.

"Not going to eat you. I promise."

Lucky still wasn't a believer. Or maybe he didn't understand English. Either way, he continued to scratch at the wall in a blind panic.

Grant clucked his tongue and pondered how to address this most recent problem. As a werewolf, he'd never been in the position where he had to comfort his food but then he never expected to be in love with someone like Lee, a fellow super predator with a soft spot for vermin. And Grant was sure of one thing: winning over this rabbit was the key to Lee's heart.

He approached Lucky slowly, dragging his feet on the wood, with his hands outstretched. As he advanced, Grant made gurgling and cooing noises he hoped sounded comforting to the rabbit's ear. When the critter belted out a shrill cry—its death scream—Grant knew his efforts were only making matters worse.

"Okay, I'm sorry," he said. "I know you must be scared."

Lucky flipped his ear.

With a sigh, Grant hunkered down on the floor. To the best of his ability, he downplayed his massive size by laying flat across the dirty wood. Likely, all he'd get for his efforts would be a fine layer of dirt and grime, but he'd pulled dumber and more demeaning stunts for lesser men than Lee. So, swallowing his pride, Grant lay flat on his belly and motioned for the rabbit to hop in his direction.

"Please, Lucky. Let's be pals—me and you. I'll feed you carrots, scratch behind your ears. How does that sound?"

Lucky twitched his ear again. His button nose—which Grant admitted was pretty cute now that they were face-to-face—twitched rapidly. But it was the way the rabbit positioned his tense body that gave Grant the most cause for concern. The damn thing's beady black eyes were fixated on the gap between him and the door, and he constantly inched in that direction as if testing the waters.

"No, no, no," he said. "Don't. Stay, rabbit, stay."

Sure enough, just as he got to his knees to block, Lucky ran right past him.

"Fuck!" Grant bellowed.

Lovestruck, also fearing for his life, he took up the chase. The additional inches of snow hindered the rabbit's panicked flight but also took its toll on Grant's already soggy, cold feet. Unlike vampires, he lacked the ability to hover above the environment, so he had to make do with his superior leg span and supernatural endurance.

Right as Grant caught up to the rabbit and dove to capture him, Lucky changed his course and darted off to the left. Instead of shouting a triumphant *gotcha!* as planned, Grant had to spit snow out of his mouth while he cussed at the painful lump forming on his knee.

There wasn't time to dwell on his failure. In this snowstorm, he'd lose Lucky in moments if he didn't stick right on his trail. Grant shot to his feet and resumed the chase, but it was too late. The wind had already scattered Lucky's scent and his tracks were invisible in the swirling snow.

Grant cussed and cussed and cussed.

What a great idea this turned out to be. Lee was bound to ram his fist through Grant's chest and rip out his lungs and heart, leaving him breathless and heartsick but not in the ways he'd hoped. Perhaps, if the fates smiled on him, Grant would at least get to see Lee holding his traitorous ribcage monster—known to others simply as the heart—before he toppled over dead.

Grant, trying his best to think of a strategy for approaching Lee, staggered back toward the shed. Unfortunately, he didn't have much time to plan. Lee, hand on his hips, hovered near the shed.

"Here you are," Lee said. "Where's Lucky?"

"Uh..."

Lee's eyes narrowed. "You know, my rabbit you said you'd eat."

"Yeah, I remember the one."

"Then tell me where he is."

Grant licked his bottom lip, which, judging from the coppery taste of blood, he'd split open during the chase. A whole bunch of excuses came to mind, each less plausible than the last. Looking Lee directly in the eye, hating the distrust he saw there, Grant spit out the truth. "He ran away."

"You mean you chased him away?"

"No, I was trying to be friends with him, and he rejected my overtures and hopped out into the night."

Lee pursed his lips and raked his gaze up and down Grant's body as if he could determine the truth of the statement using willpower alone. Vampires weren't capable of glamoring werewolves, but, right now, Grant wished it were possible. That way, Lee would know for certain Grant hadn't purposely lost the rabbit. Minus the influence of Lee's supernatural powers, Grant's words— however sincere—would probably read as lies under the present circumstances.

"I know I said some awful things, but I didn't hurt Lucky."

Lee's chin shook. "Prove it."

Chapter Twenty-Four

There was only way for Grant to prove his innocence. "Let me find him."

"How?"

"I dunno...by searching for him. Lucky is the only rabbit wearing a sweater, so he should stick out."

"Now is not the time to be a smartass."

Lee's wide-eyed indignation, accompanied by a grumpy snort, elicited an improper chuckle to add to Grant's ill-timed sarcasm sin bin. When Lee's eyebrows folded down to his customary vexed expression, Grant wondered how to best put a smile on that beloved face and a moan on those full, pouting lips. His mind also conjured all sorts of other unhelpful images; namely, Lee twining his fingers through Grant's hair and jerking him up and down on his erect cock. Someone like Lee would certainly have opinions in bed. Grant wanted to hear all of them. In detail.

Lee smacked his lips. "You're crossing me right now. And you know how much vampires hate being crossed."

"Wh—what?"

"I said we need to hurry."

"Hurry to do what?" After two seconds of enduring Lee's intense stare, Grant smacked himself. "Oh, find Lucky. Right."

"Uh-huh."

Chasing after the rabbit wasn't the group activity of Grant's dreams, but it got them cooperating and talking again, so that was something. "Okay, I need to go back and get better shoes."

To prove he wasn't trying to ditch out, Grant lifted one foot and then the other for Lee's scrutiny. The canvas fabric, a shade or two darker when wet, demonstrated the point: wearing the sneakers for too much longer might freeze his feet. Lee, no matter how angry, wouldn't allow Grant to risk his health for a bunny.

Sure enough, he clucked his tongue. "Okay, but hop on my back. I can get us back in a jiffy."

"You know how much I hate flying."

"No choice." Lee whistled and gave his back an awkward pat. "Come on, doggie."

Grant growled.

"Bad doggie. Come on. Hurry."

There was no arguing with that face, not when the mere curl of Lee's lip dug a hook in his heart and reeled him in. Resigned to his fate, Grant hopped on and wrapped his meaty tree-trunk legs around Lee's twig waist. Outsiders witnessing the scene might have worried about Lee's back with a man twice his size on top of it. Other supernaturals, those who understood the strength dynamics between werewolves and vampires, would only find the scene ridiculous.

When they sprang into the air, Grant wrapped his arms more securely around Lee's neck and held on for dear life as he zipped forward through the forest, zigzagging between the trees with a certainty that came from practice. Snow pelted Grant in the face while blasts of cold air beat against his exposed skin, stinging his cheeks and numbing the tips of his fingers and ears.

"How's it going up there?" Lee shouted over the din of the wind.

"Swell," Grant responded. "Wonderful."

"It'll be over soon. We're almost back to the hotel."

No arguing with results. Up ahead, lights from the many windows illuminated the hotel and cast a yellow glow on the ground. Eddies of snow swirled around the foundation, making the sprawling structure appear a bit like a massive ship breaking through a sea of white water.

Lee stopped. "Okay, get down. Can't be seen hauling around the enemy."

"The enemy?"

Lee shrugged. "You know...hairys."

"Werewolves." Grant growled back. "Is that what you mean?"

"Call yourself whatever you'd like, Voldemutt, but walk on your own two feet."

By now, Grant had so many different nicknames that it was difficult to pick a least favorite, but Voldemutt, the one that kick-started it all, was a pretty good contender for the crown.

"Right. Thanks."

Refusing to show his irritation, Grant smoothed his tight T-shirt down over his exposed abdomen. Lee, his expression dark, intense, unreadable, followed each of Grant's tiny movements. Confused by his friend's strange fixation, Grant lifted his shirt again to study his stomach, expecting to see a deep gash or some other noteworthy oddity marring his flesh. Blood flaked on his skin, clinging to his body's smooth, muscular planes, but his wounds had healed long ago.

Lee's eyes throbbed in time to the pulse in Grant's neck.

"Are you hungry or something?" Grant asked, lowering his voice. "You're practically stalking me."

The question snapped Lee to the present. Licking his lips in a disconcerting predatory way, he said, "I'm starving, dear heart, but why are you bleeding?"

"One of your clan decided to test poke me with his sharp claws. The wounds should heal soon."

Lee's fangs popped out. "Who?"

The corners of Grant's lips twitched, but he kept himself from smiling at Lee's sudden burst of protectiveness. Showing amusement in the face of such anger wouldn't earn Grant I'll-make-it-better kisses, which Lee generously lavished on Grant's eager body whenever he got a boo-boo. As of yet, Grant hadn't stooped to the level of purposefully injuring himself, but this was a happy accident.

Lee coughed into his hand. Eyebrow raised to the roof, he said, "You better not tell me you have an ouchie. We're not friends at the moment."

Grant perked up—not noticeably, he hoped—at the last line. A thought occurred: being enemies with Lee, if only for a bit, put him outside the friends-are-off-limits rule to romance. As a lover of details, he appreciated the spirit-but-not-the-letter distinction.

Grant let his bottom lip dip out in a small pout. "Without you, I have no one to kiss me better."

"I *know*." Lee turned away for a moment. After a deep sigh, he faced Grant. "So, who hurt you? I want names."

"Some guy with a tattoo that says 'your mouth here.'"

"Oh yes, I know him. That twerp."

"I just call him Tattoo."

"Works for me." Lee ran his tongue over his extended fangs. His eyes flashed the luminous yellow of the predator inside, and he said, "So, was this invited foreplay or did Tattoo take liberties?"

"Liberties."

"I see. Well..."

Loving the ominous way Lee's voice trailed off, not to mention the strain of his muscles under the thin barrier of his clothes, Grant stepped forward to stop him from running off to do battle. Under Grant's touch, Lee's flesh jumped. A flood of heat flushed his pale cheeks an enticing pink that Grant wanted to believe meant so many things other than horribly annoyed. Something more along the lines of *do me here and now; we're enemies, so it's okay*.

Grant leaned forward to whisper. "I'm fine. Don't worry."

"Great, but why are we whispering all of a sudden?"

The hitch in Lee's throat undercut the cool bravado he so obviously wanted to project; it forced him to say the words slowly, carefully. Those eyes of his—all the playful lights dancing—bore into Grant's. Flecks of snow clung to his long brown lashes, turning to water as he closed his eyes.

Millions of slick responses breezed through Grant's mind and tried to work their way to his tongue so that he'd come across as glib and seductive. But, as always, he picked the one most likely to make an ass out of him. "Because I don't want my heart to overhear."

Chapter Twenty-Five

As always, a whole gaggle of vampires, busy partying and making the most of their vacations, greeted them the moment they opened the door. Wearing the big grin Grant fondly remembered, Lee returned his clan's overeager affections and joined in on the inside jokes, most of them crude, circulating the room. Even Grant, who'd felt at odds with Lee's clan the entire trip, warmed to their antics.

Judging by their conspiratorial winks and knowing smiles, they assumed Grant and Lee were friends again and perhaps on the way to becoming something more. Grant's suspicions were confirmed when a vamp grabbed the crook of his elbow and whispered a side comment: "Give him the full noodle."

"Sure thing," Grant stammered.

The other nearby vampires tittered.

Grant wasn't sure if Lee overheard or not. He'd leaned against the wall near the elevator, waiting impatiently while he cleaned under his nails and pointedly ignored Grant. The damn thing had started off at the top floor and was moving at a snail's pace.

"Would it be faster to walk?" Grant asked.

"Probably."

Lee didn't budge.

Grant didn't push the issue or try to make small talk. Indeed, he hung back, hoping to keep their enemy status rolling until they made it up to the bedroom. Once the door slammed shut, Grant planned to enact operation now or never and do his best to capitalize on their hostilities. Hopefully, he'd be able to make a good case they belonged together before Lee forgave him, which was bound to happen eventually.

Tattoo walked into the room. When Lee saw him, he narrowed his eyes, flaring his nostrils for good measure. Blithely acknowledging Lee's fury, Tattoo smiled and raised his crystal glass, filled to the brim with blood, in a mock toast similar to the one he'd given Grant earlier.

Thankfully, the doors slid open before the situation turned into a brawl. To fan the flames of Lee's anger but also to make sure he didn't lunge at Tattoo, Grant jerked Lee inside the elevator and mashed the button to close the doors.

Softly, loud enough for Grant to hear, Lee hissed. At his sides, he clenched his fingers into tight fists. Hard enough to split atoms, Lee swiped at the air. The other vampire in the elevator with them, younger than most, judging by the techno-beat music wafting from his sleek headset, offered Lee a calming pat on the shoulder and a big-toothed smile. Lee, folding his arms across his chest, nodded at him and leaned backward against the wall.

"Sorry," Grant said. "I know I got a little hands-on there, but I was worried you were going to start a scuffle."

"Did you say scuffle? I bet you were old out of the box. And *I* didn't start anything."

Part of Grant thrilled at Lee's overprotective declaration, not to mention how rage brought out the animal Grant knew lurked beneath Lee's suave, too-cool-to-care vampire exterior.

Grant said, "Want to punch me out as a substitute?"

His lip curled away from his teeth. "Thinking about it, rabbit killer."

Giddy that they were still enemies, but forcing himself to appear downcast, Grant focused his eyes on the floor and thought about how best to play his hand. Obviously, tormenting Lee about the rabbit was off-limits now that Lucky was AWOL. Or maybe not.

"So, what's up with Lucky's person costume?"

"What?"

"His garb, his ensemble, his apparel." Grant listed the words, flipping his hand in the air after each one for added insult, like some smart-alecky thesaurus.

"You mean the adorable sweater I knitted for him?"

The image of Lee, fangs dangling out due to his fierce concentration, bent over a spool of yarn with knitting needles dragged a belly chuckle from Grant despite his best efforts to remain stoic. He'd always known his friend—no, temporary enemy—had a soft spot for animals. But that was a whole new level.

"What do you mean what's up with his outfit? What did it look like to you?"

"Like you dressed the plague for tea time. That's what."

Lee's teeth all came out. "You take that back."

"Vermin couture."

"Take it back!"

Grant leaned forward, almost placing his temple against Lee's, "Rodent regalia."

The swirl of color in Lee's eyes raged. Heat from his breath, which came out in quick huffs, licked the sensitive flesh under Grant's chin. Quirking his lips in a mischievous smirk, Grant bent to sniff the side of Lee's neck where his pulse should have theoretically throbbed.

Lee's subtle odor, a rainstorm on top of a swelling sea, filled his nostrils and the blood he'd been reserving for brain functioning went straight to his groin.

Ding! The doors opened.

"After you," Grant said, using his hand to keep the doors from sliding shut.

"Right." Lee shook his head. He marshaled a stern expression onto his face and stormed out of the elevator.

As Lee moved, his firm rump swished side to side like a hypnotist's pendulum. Grant's cock certainly fell under its control, stiffing against the constraints of his pants until he swore it was going to spill out over the band of his jeans.

"You're awfully quiet back there," Lee said. "And broody."

"Yup."

"Thinking of a good apology?"

Only if a good blowjob counted. And it should. "Undecided."

"Hm."

Without turning around, Lee stopped in front of the door and thrummed his fingers against the plaster wall. Grant, trying to read his mood, assessed the curve of his spine, the tilt to his head. Would he be amenable to strong hands tugging on his hips, pulling them closer together or would his eyes turn cloudy with a chance of storms the moment Grant leaned in too close?

"Okay, I don't have a key anymore, remember? You're going to have to open the door."

Feeling sheepish, Grant said, "Whoops. Forgot."

Excitement made him tremble. The hotel key, one of those slick modern cards, jittered in his hand so badly he dropped it on the floor. On his next attempt, he swiped it too quickly and the light flashed red. God, this whole thing was a really unflattering extended metaphor for his lack of sexual conquest.

"What coordination you have. Is that why you haven't been able to get your dick inside anything?"

Trust Lee to put his finger on Grant's inner thoughts.

Grant swallowed the insult and swiped the key through the lock. This time, the light turned green, indicating he'd at least successfully penetrated the defenses of his hotel room. But those weren't as well guarded as Lee's caverns, let alone his heart.

Grant stepped aside, allowing Lee to go ahead of him—not to be polite, but to get another good look at Lee's ass to remind himself what he was fighting for.

The moment Grant walked into the room, Lee whirled around. Planting one hand against the door, the other against Grant's chest, he thrust forward. The door banged shut loud enough that their neighbor pounded on the wall and shouted for them to keep it down. That bode poorly for the rest of what Grant had planned.

Apparently, it didn't pair very well with Lee's thoughts either.

"Kiss me?" Lee asked and also kind of demanded.

Chapter Twenty-Six

Plenty of smooth, seductive words lingered on Grant's lips, ready to be whispered into Lee's ear, enticing him to break the rules. All the carefully designed arguments, sweet but persuasive, turned out to be unnecessary as Lee slipped his hand under the hem of Grant's T-shirt and stroked the heated skin of his abdomen. At the light touch of his fingertips, barely solid enough to count as a graze, Grant's muscles tightened.

"Come on, kiss me," Lee said. "I know you want to."

"You said you never wanted to blur—"

"Shut up," Lee said. "We're not friends right now, you walking, talking pelt."

Right. Those had been Grant's thoughts for the entire day—to the letter—other than the talking pelt part. Why did hearing them from Lee's mouth sound so wrong, especially when his soft, full lips trembled after speaking?

Grant's mind stopped contemplating the ins-and-outs of his contradictory thoughts the moment Lee's pink tongue darted out of his mouth. He licked along the contour of his bottom lip. Empowered by Lee's blessing, Grant bent and ran his tongue along the same path.

He lifted his head to meet Lee's eyes, hoping to see his own longing reflected there. As was always the case, Lee's emotions—far more intense and on the sleeve than Grant's deep but hidden passions—radiated from the dark circle of his iris, the flushed pink of his skin, his panting breaths. He rolled his fingers in the tight fabric of Grant's black T-shirt and tugged their bodies closer.

"Kiss me," he said again. "Do it, you brute."

Tenderly, his hands almost comically large against Lee's delicate features, Grant cupped Lee's face. Using his thumbs, he stroked along the sharp contours of his chin and jaw until Lee, impatient as always, lifted himself on his tiptoes to nibble at the skin of Grant's neck. Each time his sharp teeth skimmed over Grant's sensitive Adam's apple, his heart beat faster and faster and faster. Soon, the room was only Grant, Lee, the demands of their blood, and the aches in their bodies.

"Come on, then. Come get lucky."

Growling low in his throat at the challenge, Grant closed his mouth over Lee's, letting his lips be his response since using actual words had done nothing but backfire.

Lee proved to be somewhat timid despite his earlier bravado and needling; almost shyly, he pushed back against Grant's lips, tasting him the way he sipped on fine wine but with none of the commentary (or spitting) between. Allowing Lee to set the tempo—for now—Grant forced himself to hold back.

"Are you okay with this?" Grant asked.

"Shush, worry about consequences later."

Grant sped up the kiss, gliding and pecking in a frenzy, only to withdraw and nibble at his kiss-swollen lips until Lee—always stubborn, forever the tease—opened his mouth to him. Before the gates closed, Grant swarmed, thrusting the hardness of his arousal against Lee's belly while at the same time plunging his tongue inside the warmth of his mouth.

"Grant," Lee whispered between kisses. He wiggled upward, pressing the erect line of his cock against Grant's. "God, I hate you so much right now."

Grant nibbled Lee's lower lip. "Same. You're such a damn drama queen."

Lee tangled his fingers in Grant's hair and surged against him, grinding their cocks together through the rough barrier of their clothes. "Bunny killer."

"Dracula wannabe." Grant cupped Lee's butt and mashed their bodies so close together not even a whisper of air could pass between them.

"Flea circus."

Repressing the urge to shove Lee on the bed and ride out their frustrations in a passionate frenzy, Grant slowed the pace to a maddening crawl and let himself enjoy Lee's annoyed whimpers, his relentless yet so far fruitless efforts to unzip Grant's jeans, and his occasional attempts to speed up the dance. Whenever Lee rushed forward after Grant broke the kiss, Grant pulled back, forcing their mouths to meet again on his terms and at his leisure— slow, torturous, teasing. Just like Lee deserved.

"You're like sunshine, you know that, dear heart?"

"Thanks."

"That's not a compliment. I'm a damn vampire."

Allowing himself another deep, satisfying sniff of Lee, this time along the delicate line of his collarbone, Grant snorted at the feigned venom contained in the various insults. By now, he understood such barbs hid a tender heart that Grant—if fortune smiled on him—would get to hold close to his own and keep safe.

Lee's hands had somehow managed to finally undo the top button of Grant's jeans. Triumphant, mischievous, he let loose a diabolical chuckle as his hand slid past the elastic waistband of Grant's boxers. Whatever game he was playing, he thought he was winning. And maybe he was right. Lee's cold fingers teased the heated skin near Grant's cock, nearly bringing him to his knees. As his fingers circled closer and closer to the erect flesh begging for attention—never quite getting there—Grant moaned his exasperation.

"You like that, don't you, you mangy pelt?" Lee asked.

Well, obviously. Grant couldn't say that, though. No, he had to play it at least somewhat cool. "Not as much as you're going to like this."

Channeling his inner caveman, Grant swept Lee into his arms and tossed him facedown on the bed. He landed with a thump, a slight bounce, and a sulky "hey." Grant, not wasting any time, grabbed hold of the waistband of Lee's trousers and dragged them off his body, ripping the seams in the process. Roughly, far more passionately than he would have dared with a fragile human, Grant gave Lee's butt cheek a good slap and a little nibble on the red mark his hand left behind.

"Again," Lee said, squirming upward as if he was trying to get away. Grant grabbed hold of his ankles and yanked him back down, shoving his cock against Lee's ass. "Harder," he panted.

"Okay, but only because you've been so bad."

"I *know*. Believe me, I know."

Grant tugged Lee over his lap. When his naked cock touched Grant's, which was still tucked inside his underwear, a rush of heat flowed through him. "You know you've been bad, huh? How bad have you been?"

"Very."

"And what are you going to say when you've had enough punishment?"

"Brussel sprouts."

Knowing how much Lee hated the bitter vegetable (probably why he chose it as his safe word), Grant suppressed a chuckle, which would have severely undermined the authority he was trying to cultivate. Savagely, but still mindful of Lee's limits, Grant raised his hand and brought it down with a sharp crack against Lee's ass. Afterward, he squeezed the red butt cheek, kneading it until Lee let out a whimper.

Lee wiggled on Grant's lap. "Again."

Grant couldn't let Lee dictate everything, not when he was supposedly being punished. Growling, allowing himself to sound far more menacing than he ever had, Grant shoved Lee back onto the bed. When he rolled face up, Grant flipped him back onto his abdomen.

"Come on," Lee whined. He rolled the bed sheets into tight fists. "Give it to me good. I've been so annoying."

"Don't worry. Detective Fluff is on the job."

Grant stood long enough to remove his clothes. In his haste, he tore holes in the thin fabric of his T-shirt and nearly mangled his long jeans into jean shorts. How had he managed that? He didn't know. Perhaps he'd try to figure it out later after his cock stopped throbbing and he had enough blood flowing to his head to do basic math.

Straddling Lee, Grant knelt on the bed above him. To the tune of Lee's half-hearted protests and pleas for mercy, Grant licked and nibbled the places where his hand had struck. Master of subtle hints that he was, Lee bucked his body, pressing his ass against Grant's face.

"You want something?" Grant asked.

"Please."

"Say it."

"Fine. Eat me, you mongrel."

"I'm sorry. What's that?"

"*Please.*"

Chuckling, for now ignoring Lee's request, Grant trailed kisses up and down the smooth line of his neck instead, while at the same time running the rough pads of his thumb across Lee's ass. He lapped up each of Lee's disappointed whines like they were cream. Finally, after he figured Lee had enough, Grant pulled the two cheeks apart and ran his tongue along the seam, dipping to that sweet spot and attending to it until Lee—shaking and panting—cried out.

"Grant?" Lee rolled back over. His chest quickly rose and fell. His chestnut hair, damp around his temples, clung to his flushed cheeks.

Grant lay down beside him. "Yes?"

"One criticism."

He was surprised there was only one. "Name it."

"Detective Fluff can't be your bedroom name."

Grant propped himself up using his elbow so that he hovered above Lee. For a moment, he basked in the glow of Lee's warm skin, flushed with desire, and asked himself how he'd ever been so lucky to find someone with the perfect combination of teeth and tenderness. With careful fingers, Grant plucked a strand of Lee's hair from his cheek to tuck it behind his ear, taking the extra time to smoothe the tangled strands so they fell the way Lee preferred to sparkle.

"What would you like my bedroom name to be, then?" Grant asked. "Whisper it in my ear."

Lee leaned close. Nibbling on Grant's lobe, he responded, "Shut up and fuck me."

Grant laughed. "Well, if you don't mind, Count Swear Jar, that's a nickname I'll take all night to live up to."

Chapter Twenty-Seven

Outside the storm howled as the winds battered against the walls of the hotel with all the force of a scorned lover. Inside, the heat between them lulled Grant into a placid state of contentment. Left on its own, his heart could conjure every sort of fantasy, right down to white-picket fences and puppies. Well, they'd probably end up with a cat, knowing Lee. Point was, they'd have pets, nightly walks where they'd read the stars, and all the time in the world to love.

Soon, Lee would drag him back out to the wilderness in search of the missing Lucky, Grant didn't have to be psychic to predict that dire future, and they'd drift away from each other again.

"You still mad at me?" Grant asked.

"Yes, probably forever."

Nuzzling the side of Lee's neck, where he planted several affectionate kisses, Grant considered the likelihood they'd ever do this again. The fact Lee nixed Detective Fluff as a bedroom name suggested at least one repeat performance, perhaps even two, but where would they go from there? Exactly how long would their "fight" last?

Grant's heart thudded and sent a flood of copper-tasting self-doubt to his mouth. If he hadn't needed the cantankerous organ to live—and if he hadn't wanted so badly for someone else to need it too—he'd rip the damn thing from his chest and drop kick it against a wall.

"You got a drum over there?" Lee asked. Drowsy-eyed, he blinked and yawned. He ran his fingers along the bumpy ridges of Grant's abdomen, traveling upward until he rested the flat of his hand on Grant's chest. "Your ticker says it's time."

"To?"

"Kiss me. Once to keep me, twice to let me go."

"Does that mean I can only ever kiss you once?"

Lee's smooth white skin flushed red. Those fangs of his—such playfully sharp mood stones—dented his full bottom lip when he smiled. Grant, caught in the swirl of Lee's irises, tried to slow the beat of his heart as it danced with all the colors of the aurora borealis. When Lee twined his fingers through Grant's, the feel of Lee's smooth, ageless flesh nested in his calloused grip almost tipped Grant over the edge. One more dimpled smile, another simple quip, and he'd end up in spouting-love-sonnets territory—alone.

Lee chuckled. "You got gas or something?"

Yes, heart gas. "No, just thinking."

"About?"

How much he hated having heart gas. "Us—you."

Lee smiled again. "Us-you, huh? That's quite a hybrid."

Grant tried to laugh off his awkwardness, but the noise resembled a wheeze. He curled his fist and rammed it against his lung a few times. "Sorry, got something caught in my throat."

"No worries. No need to talk. Let's lie here for a while, us and you. Sound good?"

"Sounds great."

Lee's lips curled in what Grant affectionately called his satisfied-cat face. To complete the effect, and right on cue, the green of his eyes took center stage. A thin strand of his chestnut hair fell across his cheek. Without thinking, Grant twirled it around his finger, loving how the soft strands drifted like the finest silk across his skin. He tucked it back behind Lee's ear.

"Lee?"

"Hm?"

"What's the deal with you and the rabbit? When I said I was going to eat it...well, I've never seen you so mad."

The moment Lee's eyes narrowed to slits and the contented flush along his cheeks turned an angry scarlet, Grant regretted ever opening his mouth. But it was too late to take it back. To salve the wound he'd inadvertently opened, Grant used the pad of his thumb to trace the sweet line of Lee's mouth, which trembled slightly under his touch. Thankfully, the angry color drained from his face and his tense muscles relaxed. In an instant, he reverted to the tranquil state of undeath.

"I'm sorry," Grant whispered. "I'll never do it again, but tell me why it hurt you so much."

When Lee leaned forward, the indent he left behind sucked Grant toward the middle of the bed. As he stood, he wrapped a blanket around his fair skin, drawing it over his face to hide his exposed feelings. Unwilling to let him slink away—not when there was so much pain to soothe— Grant grabbed hold of the tail end of the makeshift robe and yanked Lee back down beside him.

"Hey!" Lee tried to sound gruff, but the catch in his throat betrayed him.

"Hey nothing. Tell me."

"It's...it's nothing. I was being stupid. Sorry, forgive me for going feral on you?"

"There's nothing to apologize for other than shutting me out."

"I called you a monster. I'm so sorry, Grant."

Lee's Adam's apple bobbled when he swallowed. The urge to wrap his arms around his upset friend in a massive hug, while at the same time letting him off the hook, almost overwhelmed his common sense notion that Lee's hurt went deeper than a mere scratch. This wasn't a Band-Aid cut. This required the type of TLC only a best friend offered.

"Please, Lee. You know I'm here for you. As your friend, I—"

"Yes, I *know*, Grant. I know."

Lee's sudden outburst, punctuated by a furious foot stomp, kicked off a whole slew of contradictory thoughts in Grant's brain. More and more, he suspected Lee's feelings had evolved the same way his had. Hunting the threads of those dreams should rightly take back seat to the more pressing matter of Lee's distress. Using all his willpower, Grant shoved the myriad of questions about their relationship to the back of his mind and focused on the task at hand.

"Lee, there was something in your eyes, something I've never seen before. At least tell me you're okay?"

"Detective Fluff on the job. Doggedly determined as always."

"Doggedly? And you get after me for taking the low-hanging fruit."

Lee rolled his eyes but a small smile, which he tried to hide by slapping his hand over his mouth, peeped out from between his fingers. Merriment flickered in his eyes;

another sign the same old Lee Grant knew and loved was holed beneath the morose and secretive mask he'd worn this whole vacation. Grant only needed to dig a little further.

"There he is. There's my friend Lee. Now come tell your pal what's wrong. Is it Brian? Has he been bothering you?"

Lee snorted. "No, I don't give a damn about him or his new 'love,' what's his name."

"Then, what? Were you really that upset about the rabbit?"

"Yes, is that so hard to believe?"

"Not at all," Grant said. "You've always loved animals. But why did you get so upset when I said I'd eat Lucky? I mean...did you honestly believe I could go through with that, knowing you cared?"

Grant decided not to say, during sporadic moments of anger, he'd thought about gobbling the tiny delicious morsel in one bite and had openly boasted of his plans to do so. Also, if he were going for full disclosure, he'd admit he planned on eating other rabbits in the future. But not Lucky. Definitely not.

"Well, you're a wolf. Last I checked, not a vegetarian."

"I wouldn't eat anything you loved."

Lee swiveled his body so he faced away, a sure sign he'd teared up. "Yeah, well, it's happened before. You know, when I was going through the system. One foster thought I needed to toughen a bit, that I was far too soft for a boy, so he killed a squirrel in front of me. I'd named him Mr. Nuts. Don't laugh."

"I wasn't laughing. That's horrible."

"You don't think it's kind of funny?"

"Not at all."

"Not even a little?" Lee asked. His voice shook as he said, "The other boys in the house thought it was a laugh riot."

Grant placed a hand on Lee's shoulder. Squeezing it lightly, he let Lee know he was there without pushing for further details on what was obviously a painful memory. Lee turned back around, so quickly Grant didn't have a moment to see the tears he knew dampened Lee's cheeks, and wrapped his arms around Grant's torso, burying his face against his chest.

"I'm sorry," Lee said. "I'm sorry."

Chapter Twenty-Eight

Grant rubbed Lee's back while he hiccupped and sobbed. Wrapped in Grant's arms, with his face planted against his chest, Lee swayed back and forth as if trying to break himself from his own spell. Grant wished he'd let himself fully surrender, to cry out his frustrations without any guilt or shame. But it wasn't Lee's way to be helped. What happened to him was bullshit—he was the victim—and yet he continually apologized to Grant as though his needing support was an unwelcome burden.

"I'm sorry," Lee repeated. "I really am sorry, Grant."

"Don't apologize. Those kids were assholes and that foster should be charged."

"No, I'm sorry for ruining our vacation. I've been a real pill the entire time—Brian, the rabbit, and now this; whatever this is, it's not what I planned. Far from it."

Grant hugged him tighter. "Well, you're the type of pill that makes me feel better, so I don't mind swallowing."

"Wow, you really reached for that one; it morphed into something naughty toward the end."

"But you're smiling. I can sense it."

"No," he denied, but his voice betrayed hints of merriment, a shimmer of laughter. Seconds later, he snorted so hard it altered into a sneeze; a flood of vampire nose slime, not quite snot but close enough to be just as gross, shot onto Grant's chest. That broke Lee. He stepped back to admire his work and burst out laughing. "Let me get a towel for that. And sorry again. A sorry for every year I've been alive."

"Oh, you're laughing now, admit it—you and your toilet humor," Grant yelled as Lee vanished into the bathroom.

"Of course, dear heart. But I'm dying on the inside, so perspective."

Lee peeped his head from behind the wall's corner, looking a bit like a ground squirrel checking to see if the coast was clear. The mischievous smile Grant knew and loved so well made its reappearance, slowly spreading until his whole face radiated a whole lot of sunshine for being a vampire. "You mad?" he asked.

"No. Just waiting for the towel you promised."

Lee held it out and waved it.

"Yes, that one, princess."

"Climb to my tower, then."

Smirking—because, who was he trying to fool? He loved the chase—Grant strutted toward his friend-turned-lover, hoping the transformation would stick and this wasn't a full moon affair. He swiped the towel from Lee's outstretched hand. "Hey, thanks for nothin'."

Resting his head against the doorframe, Lee titled his head so that his chestnut hair fell over his face. Shyly, almost sweetly, he said, "Don't mention it."

Being so near Lee, especially when his naked body was a mere inch away, sent Grant on a whole new journey into fantasyland, where they woke this way every morning and went to bed each evening with their hands twined and lips meeting in a kiss. The softness of Lee's gaze, coupled with the expectant way he leaned in toward Grant, as though he were about to divulge his heart's secrets or offer a pretty sweet blowjob, had him toggling fifty-fifty on which he preferred.

"What's that sly look for?" Lee asked.

"What sly look?"

"The one plastered all over your face."

Grant made a show of turning to the mirror and of being startled by his own reflection. "Oh yes! That's my I-hope-Lee-forgot-I was-an-ass-earlier expression." He beamed. "And did you? Do you believe me when I say I won't wolf down your love bunny?"

Lee snorted. "Love bunny. Smooth."

"The smoothest."

Grant wrapped his arm around Lee's shoulder, drawing him near while praying Lee wouldn't shove him away. For once, he accepted Grant's comforting embrace without arguing or saying there was no need to make a fuss. Easily, as if they were opposite ends of a magnet, they clicked together. Grant wondered if Lee's thoughts dwelled on similar love notes or if Grant's heart would have to float a message in a bottle.

Lee lifted his hands and placed them against Grant's chest, creating a slight distance between their bodies. He traced his finger in a lazy swirl around Grant's nipple. "Grant?"

"Yeah?"

"So...there's this ball tonight..."

Yes! Grant repressed the urge to hop and click his heels together. If there were a table nearby, he probably would have tap-danced on it. Good thing the bathroom counter, cluttered with his toiletries, wouldn't hold his weight; otherwise, he might have used it as a substitute. He tried to construct a cool, confident response. Meanwhile, his mouth blurted, "I'd love to take you!"

Lee grinned, once again trying to hide it behind a curtain of hair. "Great! But that's tonight. Do you have plans for the rest of the day?"

Up in the clouds, floating in the air, Grant was far too preoccupied to be suspicious. "None that I know of. Can they include you?"

"They sure can. Let's go to the wilderness to find Lucky. Hope you brought your winter gear."

*

Grant had shifted to his quadruped wolf form to aid in the search for Lucky. Nose against the ground, he lumbered from one tree to the next, hoping by some miracle the rabbit's scent would magically float toward him and get him back to the warm hotel where there was cheesecake and possibly a bit more hanky-panky. So far, after all his efforts, he'd found a squirrel, a duck, and at least three rabbits who were not Lucky.

For Lee's sake, Grant kept at it. Whenever he thought the search was madness or that they were wasting their time, he pictured a young Lee—abused by a man who should have protected him, bullied by his foster siblings, and heartbroken over a dead squirrel that his big, undead heart wanted to love—and found his second wind.

Digging through the snow until he hit dirt, Grant followed his latest lead, which had brought Lee and him back to the shack where he'd lost the rabbit in the first place. He crammed his nose inside the tiny pocket and took a deep sniff.

Something sucked right up into one of his tender nostrils. Suppressing a yelp—he needed to be extra manly in front of Lee—Grant tried to dislodge it by slapping his paw against his nose. That only rammed it straight into his flesh. Blood rushed down his chin, mingling with his fur and turning it a muddy brown color. He transformed to a human to scream, "Shit, shit, shit."

Lee flew down from his vantage point in the sky. "What? Did you find Lucky? Is he hurt?"

"No! I sucked a pine needle into my nostril!"

Lee threw back his head and burst out laughing.

"It isn't funny!"

Lee laughed harder. "Come here, dear heart. Come here."

With his dick flapping in the wind—the universe loved to heap on the humiliations—Grant scrambled over to Lee, who placed two fingers under Grant's chin and tilted his head back. Floating to compensate for their height differences, he peered inside Grant's nose and made several odd noises that Grant couldn't quite interpret.

"Find it?" Grant asked.

"Yeah, hold still while I pluck the thing out."

Before Grant could protest, Lee poked a slender finger up Grant's nostril and pulled out the pine needle. Quick as it was, not even a one-two-after-three ordeal, Grant didn't feel a thing. "Wow, you missed your calling as a doctor."

Holding the extracted needle in front of his face, Lee smiled. "Funny you should say that. I've often thought about leaving the evil embrace of big pharma to pursue the healing arts. But, you know, the heaps of money keep me anchored to the path of sin."

"You mercenary, you."

"Well, whoever I married would be a kept man."

Playing along, at least he hoped this was part of the chase, Grant said, "And what would he have to do to win your hand?"

Lee grinned. "Get Lucky."

Chapter Twenty-Nine

Grant was pretty sure Lee meant the rabbit, not random chance, which didn't bode well for his odds. Perhaps if he staked out the locations where he'd last seen the tricky little bunny, he could swing a miracle. Or, maybe he could...

"Uh, Grant?" Lee poked his shoulder.

"Yes...yeah?"

"Are you going to shift back to wolf? Or are you trying to encourage oral by freezing your junk into a dicksickle?"

Snow swirled around his fragile human legs, piling nearly to his knee. Suddenly, the cold hit him full force and he realized he couldn't feel his toes. At this rate, he'd be lucky to escape the vacation without nerve damage. "Oh, right! Yes! Sorry, just got lost in my thoughts for a second."

Half of Lee's mouth tilted in a knowing smirk. "Next time leave a trail of bread crumbs back to your senses. Seriously, shift already. You'll catch your death."

Grant almost did as he asked but a sudden strong wind carried the scent of sunblock and cheap cologne their way. "Smell that?"

"Shift. Now."

Wide-eyed, Lee stared intently into Grant's eyes as if he were trying to subdue him or challenge him for dominance. The last bit might be exciting after they took off their clothes and wrestled. Without much effort, Grant imagined their bodies, slick and eager, grappling in the darkness. Winner takes all. But first he needed to solve the case of the pesky mischief-maker.

Lee threw his hands in the air. "Come on, you'll catch your death as a human. Stop daydreaming and shift already."

"I can't talk as a wolf. Stop nanny goating me; smell the air."

Pinching his lips, but seeing Grant wasn't about to relent, Lee twitched his nose, doing his best impression of an animal with a keen sense of smell. Grant didn't buy the con, but even a vampire, lacking the sniffing ability of a werewolf, should detect the heavy-handed mixture of odors. "You mean that foul stench?" he finally asked.

"Yes. It's the vamp who's been following us."

"You mean the carriage guy whose crime you pinned on me?"

Grant shifted to wolf to avoid an awkward conversation.

"Neat trick," Lee said. Folding his arms over his chest, he glowered at Grant in his fierce, yet adorable, rancor. "Next time you ask me to do the laundry, I'm going to turn into a bat."

Grant wagged his tail to let Lee know the plan had his full approval. Then, after a wolfy grin that he hoped came across as somewhat contrite, he cocked his head to the side, indicating Lee should follow. Bitterly complaining, Lee floated beside him, all the while keeping his eyes to the brush, the trees, the various animal burrows that were brown against an otherwise white landscape.

Lucky had to be out there somewhere. Grant promised himself he'd renew his efforts once he finished tracking the scent of the culprit, but he'd need a miracle to find one rabbit in a forest that stretched on for miles. The fact Lucky wore a hand-knitted sweater would aid Grant's search. That was the only advantage they had.

But the hunt for the mystery vamp was different, especially since their harasser helpfully followed them wherever they went.

"You on the trail of our bad guy?" Lee asked.

Grant gave him a brief nod but immediately resumed his tracking. Nose constantly twitching, he flitted here and there, allowing the smells, not his eyes, to guide his path. He blundered into a low-hanging branch, which tangled in his long fur and pulled so hard it pinched. When he yanked free of the branch's grasp, a large tuft of his fur—his magnificent coat—twisted out and drifted to the ground.

"Don't poke out your eye," Lee drawled from behind. "Your vision is already impaired."

Grant snorted at the barb, mostly because he couldn't formulate an adequate response with wolf vocals and shifting back to human might indeed freeze his dick off.

The trail, so fresh Grant swore he smelled what the culprit had for lunch, stopped against the north wall of the hotel. Grant tilted his head upward, hoping to catch a glimpse of a fleeing suspect, but a fat drop of water from the snow melting on the eaves splattered against his nose instead. Of all the eaves in the world, he had to stand under the leaky one.

"Are we going up?" Lee asked. "Hot pursuit or whatever it's called?"

Hopping on Lee's back in wolf form was out of the question. But he could carry him.

Grant nodded.

"Are you going to shift back to human?"

Grant shook his head. He raised his front paws off the ground and rested them on Lee's shoulders.

"Seriously? You want me to lift you and zip you to the roof?"

Grant wagged his tail.

"Oh, dear heart. You are a chore. But all right, if I must."

In a flash, Lee swept Grant off his feet and made a beeline straight for the top. Windows blurred. The ones with the curtains open displayed intimate scenes from other lives. The dioramas flashed past his eyes, like he was flipping through stations to find something good to watch. By the time they soared to the top, Grant, whose stomach lurched while doing backflips in his throat, was seconds away from spewing out everything he'd eaten the entire week and possibly a burrito from a past life.

Barely disturbing the snow, which was heavily packed on top of the flat roof, Lee hovered and scanned the area. "No footprints, no one around," he said. "Smell anything?"

Grant shifted back to human to say, "Yeah. We're close. Let's go back down the other side."

"Roger that."

The moment they landed on the ground, Grant shifted to wolf and lumbered through the snow to the area where the odor beckoned him. Suddenly, he caught a whiff of another familiar scent. Lucky. The rabbit. Oh, this wasn't fair. Not at all.

"What's wrong?" Lee asked him.

Only that he had to choose between two demands from his id—his prey drive or his sex drive. Grant paced between the two, trying to make up his mind as the trail from each grew colder and colder. Soon, the wind and the freezing temperatures would rob him of either choice. Indecisiveness cost time and both of his marks were fleet-footed and elusive.

"Make a move," Lee said, sounding bored. "Vampires move fast."

Grant wanted to throw his hands in the air and cuss up a storm, but his hands were paws and he was already wading through the last bit of snowfall, so he sent the problem to his heart. It had a decision back to him in a blink.

He indicated Lee should follow by tilting his head to the side. The tired roll of Lee's eyes matched Grant's mood to the letter, but he wouldn't submit to groans and teeth gnashing with so much on the line. He'd focus. He'd close the case. He'd win this game.

The closer they got, the more apprehensive Grant became.

Lucky's sweater, the one Lee had hand knitted him, hung from a branch. Happily, the rabbit had managed to wiggle free. Unfortunately, there was no sign of the lottery ticket to Lee's heart. Not even a trace of Lucky remained, which seemed like a cruel jab after he'd raised his hopes to impossible highs.

"You came after the rabbit?" Lee asked.

Grant nodded. He stuck his nose through the crest of the snow. He didn't hit any new leads, just the smell of old droppings, dirt, and cigarette butts. Not exactly a bouquet he wanted to rub all over his body, but what was really galling was how it reeked of failure.

Lee cleared his throat. A big smile, complete with fang dimples on his delicious lower lip, graced his face. Grant waited forever for him to say something, anything really, but he simply repeated, "You chose the rabbit."

No, Grant wanted to say. *I chose you.*

Chapter Thirty

Lee's voice tilted in a manner Grant would describe as chipper as he babbled about Lucky's great escape from his city clothes. "That's what I was worried about. That he'd get it caught on something and end up strangling himself. I dwelled on it; it clawed my insides. I knitted him the damn thing. It's a load off my mind, you know?"

Grant nodded. It was all he could do until they made their way back to the warmth of the hotel where he could shift back to human. Then, he'd take Lee in his arms and they'd dance the night away under the dimmed lights of the hotel's ballroom. After that, well, he'd satisfy his prey drive and his sex drive in one swoop.

"What's your tail wagging about?" Lee asked.

God, Grant was so glad to be in wolf form right now. Otherwise, he'd be stuck answering the awkward question with his equally awkward voice, which would shake with his excitement. Stuck in his wolf form, he hid behind a toothy grin and another enthusiastic tail wag. Let Lee debate the meaning of the gestures. A little suspense might whet his appetite so he'd be salivating by the time Grant made another move.

The doorman nodded at them as they walked through the front doors of the hotel. Lee waved in response. For once, no gaggle of vampires greeted them. There were a few scattered here and there, most lounging on the velvet-covered couches or leaning against the walls, their heads bent in conversation. Each gave Lee a knowing wink or a cocky sideways grin as they strolled through the lobby. Heat stained Lee's cheeks red. Although his friend hovered at least a foot off the floor, Grant swore he staggered. Perhaps swayed would have been a better word. Either was impossible. Always graceful, Lee never missed a beat.

"Are you going to shift?"

Was he kidding? Grant couldn't quite tell.

"They've seen your junk already, and I hear you promised them you'd show more butt. Also, we have some things to discuss."

The last bit sounded ominous, discussing things had led to at least five breakups in Grant's past, but they needed to be open about his feelings. No more hiding the depths of his affections or repressing the impulses of his heart in order to avoid tripping Lee's alarms. He'd tiptoed around for far too long.

"Well?" Lee prompted him.

Grant shifted to his human form. "I'm all yours. What's on your mind?"

"We're still friends, aren't we?" Lee asked.

"Until the Earth is salt."

"Good. Good. It's just you haven't said much about last night."

"I've been in wolf form most of the day. We were looking for Lucky, if I recall."

Lee offered a half-tilted smile, directed toward the floor rather than at Grant, in response to the reminder. Shyly, perhaps even a bit guiltily, he toed the floor; the marble squeaked under the rubber of his soles. Lee jumped at his own noise, and Grant hid his amusement by covering his mouth and coughing.

"On edge about something?" Grant asked, hoping the answer was yes and praying the source of their anxieties was the same. It would be just his luck to blurt out his concerns about their date tonight and their future only to find out Lee had forgotten to mail off his taxes or something equally mundane. That couldn't be it. The nervous ticks, the shy blushes, the way Lee peeked at Grant's naked body whenever he thought he could get away with it undetected.

"Yeah, I'm worried about a lot of things. Mostly, I want to know where we stand."

"What do you mean?"

"Well, we had sex and then I cried about my childhood dead-squirrel trauma."

At the reminder of the cruelty Lee suffered, Grant's lips pinched into a frown. "I'm glad you told me."

"Well, I've made this vacation into a torture wheel. I want to make it up to you tonight. That's what I'm trying to say."

Although the promise in Lee's words, coupled with the silky tenor of his voice, sent a hot rush of blood to his nether regions, Grant balked at the idea Lee was somehow to blame for any of his troubles. "You don't owe me anything. And I ruined my own vacation. I've been too preoccupied with—"

"With?"

"Matters of the heart. I guess I'm the dumb guy in each tragic play after all, and that's my fatal flaw."

Lee opened his mouth to respond, but a sudden crack above their heads jarred them both out of the conversation. Seconds later, a large planter from one of the floors above hurled down toward them. Air whistled around the heavy object, but Grant didn't have time to react before it slammed into the floor mere inches from his feet. The marble cracked, fanning out like a spiderweb from the epicenter of the impact site. Dirt erupted out of the heavy concrete planter as it tilted on its side and rolled, stopping when it hit a nearby wall with a loud crack.

"What the hell?" Lee asked. He lifted his foot to shake off some of the dirt that had landed on the glossy leather of his shoe.

"Our mischief-maker is escalating."

Instead of answering, Lee shot up from the damaged floor of the hotel, flying at a speed Grant would have thought impossible, even for a vampire. He landed on the balcony above with a snarl so loud that even the vampire running the front desk looked away from the wreckage the planter left behind to glower. To Grant, he said, "This hotel doesn't want further trouble. Better stop your friend before he makes things worse and just let me call the police."

"I am the police," Grant muttered, but he took the vamp's message to heart.

Grant couldn't fly, but he could run pretty fast as a wolf. He shifted and bolted for the stairs. As he rounded the corner, his padded feet skidded on the slick marble, polished to perfection with a glossy, slick coating that his claws scratched. Grant thumped against the wall, which, happily, at least stopped him from sliding farther away from the stairs.

Locked onto Lee's scent, caring more about finding his friend in one piece than finding their perpetrator, Grant skipped as many stairs as possible, throwing his full weight into maintaining a strong forward momentum as he charged upward.

"Hey!" a vampire yelled as Grant breezed past him. "Watch where you're going!"

Under normal circumstances, Grant's embarrassment for his rude behavior would have stopped him in his tracks, and he would have offered the offended party an apology. Now, he didn't so much as give the offended vamp a second glance. Instead of slowing his pace, he sped up. Rather than watch where he was going, Grant continued to follow his nose, fully committing himself to the reckless chase. Beneath him, his paws thundered almost as loudly as his heart.

He stopped on the floor where Lee had landed and shifted back to human. "Lee? Where are you?"

No response.

Grant followed his friend's trail with his nose. As the strong stench of cologne and sunblock mixed with Lee's familiar and subtle rain scent, Grant's heart sped its pace, pounding so hard it began to ache like a sore muscle.

"Lee?" he called again. "Lee?"

A groan caught his attention. Grant whirled in the direction of the noise, charging heedlessly forward until he saw Lee. Propped against a wall, blood dripping from a wound on his brow, he groaned as Grant knelt beside him but didn't open his eyes or give any indication he knew Grant was there.

Grant shook him. "Lee? Can you say something?"

Lee's eyelids fluttered, suggesting that perhaps he heard, but he didn't respond to any of Grant's questions. The cadence of his breathing sped and slowed down in his strange slumber. Not knowing what else to do, Grant lifted him and carried him to safety.

Chapter Thirty-One

Grant lay Lee on top of the bed they'd shared at the start of their vacation, pausing to draw the blankets to his chin since he'd been shivering—whether from the cold or some hidden torment, Grant couldn't tell. He assumed the latter and worried incessantly about how he was going to dispel the enchantment keeping Lee under its thumb. The odd comatose state reeked of vampire powers far beyond what Grant had ever encountered, which didn't bode well for his odds of finding a quick solution.

"Hold on," he said as he gently tucked a loose strand of hair behind Lee's ear. Using the back of his hand, he stroked Lee's cheek and clucked in concern at the fevered heat radiating from his skin. "I'm going to get what help I can."

In the dim light, the floating dust particles gave the room a grainy black-and-white movie feeling. Grant couldn't help but think of old detective movies, the type where the protagonist smoked like an industrial village and called women dolls, as he dialed the station on the hotel's retro rotary phone.

Officer Bauer, always upbeat but never on his beat, answered. "What can I do for you?" he asked after identifying himself.

"It's Grant Porter. I need supernatural officer backup at the Grand View Hotel. Someone is stalking me and my friend; he made an attempt on our lives."

Officer Bauer, clearly grasping the seriousness of the situation, whistled sharply. Afterward, he added, "Gosh, that's terrible, Grant."

After a long period of silence, which should have lasted mere seconds before he was transferred to the lieutenant of the supernatural force, Grant said, "Yes, thank you for your sympathy, Officer Bauer. Can you please direct my call?"

"Sure thing!"

Everything about the world contrived to piss him off today. At least that's how Grant decided to interpret the horrible slog of elevator music he had to endure before someone picked up the call. At least the other voice on the line—crisp and direct—suggested a veteran officer rather than a rookie cop fresh out of school and green as a sapling. It took him a bit to recognize Lindsey, who made it a habit to avoid contact outside of work.

"Grant Porter here," he told her. "I'm a local PI having a bit of supernatural trouble at the Grand View Hotel."

Briefly, he recapped the events of the last few days to the dispassionate Lindsey, who only occasionally interrupted his report to ask brisk questions, which he answered with expert efficiency. The easy back-and-forth was a welcome change after all the hesitation, the galling uncertainty of the last few days. Grant was relieved that when called to duty he could still behave as a disciplined, seasoned detective with a head full of facts and details rather than a cloud of Lee's rainwater scent.

"I can send a vamp officer there, but he may not arrive for at least a day," Lindsey told him. "There are closer places to dispatch if you require immediate assistance."

"I need a vampire to deal with my perp," Grant told her. "Or someone who can remove powerful glams."

On the other end of the line, her fingernails tapped against her desk. The sensitivity of her mic magnified the noise to almost unbearable levels. Grant moved the phone away from his ear, wincing as she continued to drum. He hoped Lindsey came to a conclusion soon; he wasn't sure he'd withstand another minute of the racket without snapping. And that would be unfortunate. Allowing his temper to get the better of him didn't suit his cause. Besides, Lindsey didn't deserve the harshness; she was doing the best she could, given the scarcity of supernatural cops on staff.

"Look, I understand you can't conjure a vampire who can remove charms out of thin air. All I ask is that you put the nearest one en route."

"Of course, Porter. I'm looking for possible responders in our database. We have a few civilian consultants, mostly PIs like yourself, scattered here and there. One might be able to help you remove the glam."

Grant pressed his fingers into a steeple and gave thanks to Saint Lindsey, who might see him clear of this disaster after all. Behind him, Lee moaned and flailed. The bed sheets twisted around his legs, bunching to the point he struggled to move. Persistent beyond Grant's comprehension, even in a magical coma, he struggled until he managed to shove them to the bottom of the bed, and then he kicked them off from there.

"Are you still there, Porter?" Lindsey asked.

"Yes. Yeah. Sorry. My friend was distressed."

"Is he in stable condition, Porter?"

"I believe so, but it's hard to tell."

"Well, bizarre coincidence, but it seems one of our favorite vampire consultants is actually at the hotel with you. At least, he indicated that's where we could reach him for the next week in the event of an emergency."

Grant gave his changing luck a celebratory fist pump. In his enthusiasm, he even forgot to maintain rigid formality. "That's terrific! How can I contact him?"

"I will brief him on the situation and pass along your room number. Update me within the hour. For now, I'm dispatching a human officer to your location."

After the exchanged information, the line went dead without so much as a goodbye or a thank you. Grant sat at the foot of the bed to wait for the mystery vampire consultant to show, hoping he'd arrive before Lee accidentally hurt himself. Grant feared he'd bang his head on the sharp edges of the night table if he were left on his own.

"Help is coming any minute now," Grant said.

Grant cupped Lee's cheek in his massive hand to steady his convulsions. Whenever it appeared his thrashings were becoming panicked, Grant whispered assurances in his ear, thinking, if Lee heard him, he might take comfort in knowing he wasn't alone. Lee's eyelids fluttered again, but his tense muscles relaxed and his erratic breathing stabilized to a steady rise and fall of his chest.

Someone tapped on the door. The noise was so light, so ethereal that Grant might have missed it if he weren't a werewolf. He hoped this meant the consultant would be easy to deal with, perhaps even shy if there was such a thing as a bashful vampire.

"Coming," he shouted, earning him another heavy thud on the wall from the guy in the room over. To Lee, he whispered, "See, the consultant is here. We'll get you back on your feet in no time."

His optimism faded the moment he recognized the vamp on the other side of the door—Tattoo. Smiling with all his sharp teeth, he said, "Hiya, beautiful."

Chapter Thirty-Two

Grant, halfway tempted to slam the door shut in Tattoo's face, suppressed an enormous groan and forced the uncooperative muscles in his face to lift in something resembling a smile. "Hiya," he said back.

"Nailing the whole social graces thing. I believe you're super happy to see me."

Tiredly, Grant rubbed the back of his head. "So, you're actually the consultant?"

"Afraid so, big fella. Going to let me inside? I mean, I've been inviting you for days, but maybe that was never your scene."

"Ha. Funny."

Grant stood back. By sweeping his arm, he gestured for Tattoo to breeze right on past, which he did with a big gotcha grin smeared all over his face. Grant sniffed him extra hard, wishing on a star that he'd detect any trace of sunblock or cheap cologne on his skin. He didn't know what he'd do if he hit pay dirt, especially since he needed the persistent sexual sadist to break Lee's glamor, but he wanted the emotional satisfaction of finding his perp and it being someone he disliked.

"Hey, Mister Snarly, thinking about using your teeth?" Tattoo asked. "Because you know I'd be into that."

Grant snorted. "Lee's over there. Can you help him or not?"

"Probably." Tattoo wiggled his fingers in front of Grant's face. "Now go away. Go be a tower princess hunk over in the corner."

Grant, suppressing a whole legion of sarcastic comments, flopped down in the nearby swivel chair and monitored Tattoo as he poked and prodded the unconscious Lee. Occasionally, he'd *hmm* and *aha* as though onto something, but if he discovered any relevant information in the course of his checkup, he didn't share.

"Don't interrupt," Tattoo said when Grant started to speak.

With a snap of his jaw, Grant closed his mouth and brooded in the corner as previously instructed. He stressed over how Lee would react knowing Tattoo was running his hands up and down the contours of his body in a way that struck Grant as overly familiar. Not that he was territorial. No, no, no. He already knew how Lee would feel about any possessiveness; all snarly teeth with very little soft nibbles. And Grant wanted all the soft nibbles. Yes, those most certainly belonged to him. If those nibbles were a tree, he'd pee on them. Not in a territorial way. Because he wasn't that. No, no, no.

"Are your thoughts babbling in your ear?" Tattoo asked. "If your brow hangs any lower, I'll stumble on it."

Grant hopped in his seat. From what Lee told him, vampires couldn't read thoughts, but Tattoo eerily put his finger right on the pulse of Grant's mood. Grant, uncomfortable under scrutiny, squirmed in his seat. "Are you and Lee close? You're from the same clan, so I assume you at least know each other."

"We're friendly, though sometimes we like to compete." Tattoo graced him with another of his cocky grins. "Why the keen interest? I swear your eyeballs move with my hands."

"It's just you're touching his..."

"Stomach?"

"Yes."

"And that bothers you, does it?"

"No," Grant said, really meaning yes.

"Well, obviously you're cool with it." Tattoo laughed breezily as if to show himself wiser than his words. Then, suddenly serious, he said, "Lee got walloped with a powerful glamour. He's deep under."

"I didn't know vampires could charm their own."

"Yes, such a spell takes one very old, not to mention powerful, vampire. There are few able to accomplish such a feat, myself included."

Trying not to sound suspicious of the note of pride, essentially a boast, in Tattoo's voice, Grant asked, "Can someone as powerful as you undo it?"

"Of course. With the proper motivation."

The mischievous light in his eye, so full of confident swagger, suggested proper motivation meant what fell between the lines, which Grant read easily enough, especially in light of their past history. To hammer home the point, which he didn't need to do, Tattoo floated toward Grant and mashed their bodies together, grinding where their pelvic bones met. He curled his fingers through Grant's thick black hair and tried to tug their mouths together.

Grant pulled away. "I thought I made myself clear enough before."

"Oh, you did. You did. But now you need me as much as I need you. I'll take my payment up front," he purred. "Otherwise, Sleeping Beauty over there will have to wait for another prince's kiss."

"How will he stay safe without me here and—"

"I'll put up a quick protection spell."

The secluded venue limited his options. It wasn't like he could call dispatch and have them send another powerful vampire to remove the glamour and have Lee up and about before sundown. He'd been lucky enough to have Tattoo here, available and eager to help, but for a price.

Meaningless sex was what Doctor Lee prescribed at the start of this little vacation; Grant would only be following his orders. Why, then, did it sound like a small betrayal when he said, "Sure, fine. Whatever gets Lee back on his feet. Just let me call the office back to let them know the situation is handled."

"Good." He patted his knee. "Come on, then. Let's go to my room."

*

Tattoo stopped at his hotel door. "Great, now that you're here, go ahead and leave."

"What?"

"Toodles."

"Are you...are you kidding me?"

Smiling to show off the sharp points of his incisors, Tattoo waved him off again. He turned his back to swipe his key card through the lock, *ahaing* when it buzzed. Once again, he graced Grant with one of his trademark smirks, so full of confidence and sly humor.

Trying his best to hide his impatience, Grant said, "Is it time to take care of Lee then?"

"Already taken care of, actually. He should wake soon."

"You neglected to mention that earlier."

Tattoo shrugged. "My bad."

"Then what was the point of this? Why lead me to your room?"

As Grant's ire increased, Tattoo's amusement rose to correspond. By the time Grant wanted to punch a hole in the wall, the aggravating vampire was practically tap dancing in the hallway. His gaze raked over Grant's stiff body, head to toe, before meeting his eye again. Winking, he said, "I honestly just wanted to see if you'd do it. You're a loyal guy, you are. I've been watching you, testing you."

Grant didn't know what to make of any of those strange confessions, other than to seethe and do his best to keep his temper from curling his fingers into a fist. Getting into a fight wouldn't help Lee, and *that* had to be his priority. Heat radiated off his skin. Smiling tightly, Grant said, "Is this the end of it, then?"

"Sure is. Thanks for the good times, Noodle. Be sure to give Lee my best."

Chapter Thirty-Three

Excitement kick-started Grant's good cheer into high gear. The golden vases filled to the brim with flowers in the hotel's lobby reminded him less of a funeral home, the banter, and the quibbling, of Lee's raucous clan chimed like bells to his ear, and the apple he nibbled on to quell his gnawing hunger tasted less of purgatory and more like a fat steak in heaven.

With a spring in his step and a cheesy song playing in his doubly cheesy heart, Grant wove through the crowd of vampires on his way to meet Lee. They had a big date tonight, and he was optimistic they'd have a lot to gab about before and after. All signs pointed to shared feelings; Grant's romance sniffer couldn't be so far off track, not when Lee's hints bordered on declarations.

"Sir," the vamp at the front desk said, waving his arm to flag him down.

"Yes?"

"You have a message, sir."

Smiling, Grant snapped it out of his fingers. "Thanks!"

"No problem, sir. Oh, the gentleman who left the message said he was the backup you requested. Sorry to barge into your business, but I thought you should know more officers are in route. The hotel reported the incident too."

Some good news at last. "Thank you for letting me know."

Grant flipped open the folded piece of paper and read the scribbled note: Room 409. Please touch base ASAP.

The stalker issue, forever plaguing their cursed vacation, sapped some of his high energy. Sooner or later, he'd have to get on the hunt; this time seeing it through to the end, Lee's feelings and Lucky's safety be damned. Normally, he'd be salivating at the opportunity to get on the trail of the bad guy—he lived for the chase, but today it was only an unpleasant chore he had to see through until he held Lee in his arms.

He knocked on the door to his own hotel room. Tattoo said Lee should be awake by now, but Grant knew better than to startle a vampire, even if that vampire was his soon-to-be sweetie pie. He couldn't trade oral with his throat ripped open, at least not to their mutual pleasure. "Lee, it's Grant. Are you awake?"

"Yes, come in."

Grant swiped his card. When the light turned green, he used his shoulder to push the door open. He tossed the card on the counter and strolled into the bedroom. Lee, his back turned and his legs dangling over the edge of the bed, didn't greet him or even acknowledge his existence.

"Hey," Grant said. "Feeling better?"

Lee kept his back turned. "This entire room smells like Tattoo, the vampire who's been courting you the entire trip."

Oh no, Grant wasn't going to let this chestnut derail their future happiness. "Nothing happened. He said he'd been 'testing' me, whatever that means. And his smell is in here because he's the one who broke the glamour. Don't be ridiculous, you know I…"

"I know you…"

Shit, Grant needed the moment he said the words to be special, not something he blurted to defend himself against ridiculous accusations. "You know I don't go for his type."

"Right."

Grant plopped himself on the opposite side of the bed; his bulk bent the mattress, bringing them closer together. After tonight, there'd be no more dancing around the obvious, just dancing. And necking. And laughing. And maybe their own kid to terrify with ribbons of Twizzler blood. They had a lot of time to pick and choose from an infinite number of ands.

Grant put his hand on Lee's shoulder. "Now answer me…are you feeling better?"

"Yes, except for the whole Tattoo thing."

"Okay, well then don't run off and get yourself entranced, and I won't ever talk to him again." Grant tweaked Lee's nose. "Now, I know you have precious little patience for my detective stuff, but I have to ask what you remember about the attack. I called in backup, and I need to meet with them soon. Your statement would help."

"I don't want you to leave this room."

"Not an option. Give me everything you can remember."

"I remember my good friend PI Fluff spends most of his time chatting with the locals and finding missing persons. Even when you were on the force, you never pulled your gun. You're a private investigator now, not some Dirty Harry. Stay here with me where it's safe."

His pride ached at the description of his job. Was that really how Lee thought of him, as some puffed-up gossipy security guard who fled at the first sign of danger? True enough that he'd never pulled his gun when he was on the force and his duties as a community officer weren't ever high-risk, but he'd responded to a lot of calls for backup where he had to dash headfirst into a nasty fray. Grant didn't look for opportunities to prove his mettle, but he also hadn't ever shirked from his duties.

"Oh, dear heart, I know you're no coward," Lee said, guessing at his thoughts. "Make the hotel deal with the issue. They must have phoned in the incident by now."

Grant admitted, "They did. But I have a job to do. What do you remember?"

Lee's eyes narrowed. "Nothing."

"Lee, really now."

"I don't want you to leave when a vampire powerful enough to put me under is running amuck."

Lee tilted his head so his chestnut hair shrouded his expression. Knowing him, he hid a whole slew of worries, doubts, and possibly tears that he'd go to his undeath bed denying ever rolled over his perfect pale cheeks.

More gently this time, Grant asked, "What do you remember, Lee?"

"The answer really is nothing, Grant. That's why I'm so terrified for you."

Chapter Thirty-Four

Surprised to see the face of an officer he didn't recognize—odd, but not impossible given he'd been off the force for a year—Grant stood at the open door and considered the newcomer, who he didn't quite trust at first sight. The officer, rail thin and dressed slovenly in jeans and a flannel shirt, graced him with a mocking half salute and then went back inside the hotel room, where the television blared, without so much as a second glance or an introduction.

"You must be Grant," he said. Although the hotel had a no-smoking policy, he balanced a cigarette, burned down almost to the nub, between his fingers.

"Yes, and you are?"

"Ready to get this over with."

"Glad we share similar goals, now what's your name?"

"Charlie."

Tiredly, Charlie took a long drag from his cigarette, afterward releasing a circular puff of smoke into the otherwise pleasant air. He waved his hand in front of his face to shoo the acrid fog away from his nose, directing it toward Grant, as though the slight gesture would ward off cancer. Then, he flicked the butt against the wall. Showing complete disrespect, he flopped down on the bed and considered Grant with a strange grin that hinted at amusements he didn't bother to explain.

Grant picked up the discarded butt. After properly snuffing it, he tossed the cigarette in the garbage bin and prepared himself for a rough ride with an officer who didn't take to saddle.

"Well done. You're the finest supernatural PI this side of the hemisphere. Maybe you can collect litter in the park next."

Grant let the intended insult, which actually seemed like a better idea to serve the people, roll off his back. Remaining standing, inching toward the door, he said, "Let's get moving. There are witnesses to interview. You know how quickly the information fades."

"In a bit. I'm watching some cable on the department's dime. You seen this show?"

From the groans, moans, and the sound of wet, rhythmic sucking, Grant already knew Charlie was talking about porn. He refused to turn his head to confirm though. "You said you wanted to get this over with. Sitting at the television doesn't help matters."

Charlie shrugged. "Not to your taste, huh? Maybe if it was a couple of cocksuckers?"

"Not even then."

Snorting in laughter, Charlie grabbed the remote control. He fumbled around with the buttons, hitting all of them except the big red one and laughing the entire time as though he was playing a fun game. At first, Grant suspected Charlie was messing with him, dragging out the ordeal as some dull show of power that men like him believed put them above others. But it was worse than that. He was drunk.

Grant didn't expect the best and brightest to be sent to this far place, at this late hour, or for a mere stalker with murderous tendencies, but he regretted ever putting in the call if his whistle attracted this dog.

"Well," Grant said. "I'm off without you. Enjoy your show."

"Don't leave in a huff, princess. I'm almost done. By that, I mean—"

"Yes, I guessed at what you meant. That's why I'm leaving."

After a heavy sigh, which Grant threaded with as much distaste as his normally immaculate manners allowed, he pivoted on his heel and made to leave.

He didn't get very far.

From behind, a heavy hand thundered against Grant's skull, striking him in that sweet spot right above the neck, forcing him to pitch forward into the wall. With a sharp crack he prayed wasn't bone, Grant hit the wall and then slumped to the floor. Not quite unconscious, but seeing swirls of light in his vision that announced an oncoming blackout with fanfare, Grant looked into Charlie's leering face right as his boot lifted.

"It's rude not to let men finish," Charlie said and struck.

*

Sparks of color flared behind Grant's eyelids, bright and festive as fireworks but also a billion times more nauseating. Beneath him, the floor tilted but he credited the dizzy sensation to low blood sugar rather than the throbbing spot where Charlie struck him. The last was as much a blow to his pride as to his head, but only one drew blood.

"You're awake."

Grant didn't recognize the gruff tone, which had a tickle of French that sounded affected. He tried to peer through the darkness to study the face behind the drawl, but a blindfold clouded his vision so that he could only discern the vague outline of a white man with sandy-blond hair. The finer details of his features blurred through the dark fabric, rendering him as unrecognizable as his voice. Whoever he was, this was the mischief-maker in the flesh. The lingering traces of sunblock and the overwhelming stench of the cologne marked him as the source of Grant's woes.

"How are you feeling?" the man continued when Grant didn't reply. "I hope your injury isn't too severe."

The mischief-maker strolled toward Grant. Even as he bent down, pressing their faces close together, Grant couldn't observe anything to identify the man—no brow slope, nose shape, or eye color stood out amidst the wash of white of his face. Either Grant needed to go to the eye doctor, assuming he managed to survive this ordeal, or the mischief-maker channeled an enchantment to work alongside the blindfold to obscure his vision.

Tsking, the mischief-maker swiped his hand across Grant's brow, pulling his hair where it had matted in the dried blood. Another sharp tug reopened the wound; blood dripped along Grant's brow, rolling along the slope of his forehead until it pooled at the seam of his blindfold. The wet spot of fabric clung to his forehead.

"Goodness, Charlie knocked you a good one, didn't he?"

Grant only grunted in response.

The mischief-maker slapped him across the cheek, hard enough to make the side of his mouth swell and tingle. "Manners. Now, let me ask you if you called any other backup? Supernaturals? Human officers? The military. Whatever. Spill. Who else is coming—if anyone?"

Through the tirade, most of the accent got lost; Grant recognized the unmasked version of the voice from somewhere, but he couldn't quite pin a face or name to it. This was one of those unfortunate tip-of-the-tongue moments where the answer flashed briefly, only to vanish in his brain's memory file.

Grant's delay earned him another slap. This time, he tasted blood and felt the sting and the burn from a long trail of scratches that bled along his cheek. Mischief-maker screeched, "Answer me!"

"No one else is coming," Grant said. "I'm on my own, so do what you're going to do."

Mischief-maker stood. In a tone that was once again condescending and pleasant, he said, "Don't be so arrogant. You're not even my target."

"Who—" Grant stopped himself before he finished his question. He knew there was only one answer, and it tied a knot inside his guts and pulled. "Leave Lee alone," he whispered. "Do whatever you want to me, but leave him alone."

The mischief-maker snickered. "Oh, I'll leave him alone—when I'm done with him."

Chapter Thirty-Five

Nearby, a lone guard leaned against the wall as he chomped on a crisp apple and hummed lightly to himself as though he were there waiting for a hot date rather than guarding a prisoner who happened to be a werewolf. Judging by his smell—that faint yet unmistakable whiff of undeath, which mangled with the tartness of the apple— the guard was a vampire, who often thought of werewolves as big, dumb dogs instead of threats. To take advantage of that arrogance, assuming the guard suffered from it, Grant would first need to free himself.

Hoping the coils of rope might fray and eventually snap with enough pressure, Grant rubbed the bindings against the splintering wood of the post to which he was tied. Since his guard possessed hearing at least equal to his own, Grant didn't bother masking the noise or pretend to be doing anything other than trying to escape. There was no point in playacting when his guard's supernatural abilities easily detected any subterfuge. He curbed his urge to shift to wolf. Whatever else, that would earn him an instant reaction.

Happily, the guard only chuckled at his attempt. Yawning, he said, "Good luck with that."

"Thanks," Grant muttered.

After a while, Grant conceded the guard had a point: his efforts were ridiculously ineffective and sawing his restraints against the wooden post, at least so far, only yielded him splinters lodged into his wrists and rope burn, neither of which made the situation better.

But what else was there to do but struggle to escape? Nothing. He couldn't give up hope and leave Lee to his fate. Lee. Thinking the name alone dulled the pain in his wrists. Grant doubled his efforts.

Through the blindfold, he glimpsed the outline of the guard as the vamp paced from one end of the room to the next, still chewing his apple while he hummed the same cheery tune that sounded a bit like the theme to Excalibur when Grant set his imagination to it. Suddenly, the guard stopped, sharply turning his body in Grant's direction as though he detected a threat. Grant strained his ears, but heard nothing; he twitched his nostrils but smelled nothing.

"What's this now?" the guard asked. "Some friend of yours?"

Not that Grant knew of, but he hoped there might be another officer out there searching for him, preferably a supernatural who would be a match for their enemies. Otherwise, whatever human sap they sent would most likely be tied to the post along with Grant in an instant. Or worse.

"Answer me," the guard snapped. "Who do you have coming?"

"No one. But I wouldn't tell you if I did."

The guard snorted at that. "Okay, well, you stay here, sunshine. I'm going to go take a look-see. Keep a spot warm for me while I'm gone."

"Will do," Grant responded with equal irony.

After the guard had gone, Grant resumed his battle to break free from his restraints. Free from supervision, he shifted to wolf. Massive now, his bulk thrust full force against coils, which, rather than retreating or snapping, dug into his flesh, seemingly cutting all the way to bone. Repressing a howl of pain, Grant thrashed and ignored the flow of blood washing over his hands. Splatters of it hit the ground with daunting regularity. With each surge, the flow increased. At least the blindfold had fallen off. Mild progress was better than no progress at all.

Easy. Don't panic. Slow and steady.

Grant closed his eyes, breathing deeply and evenly against the pain. Blackness swirled around his outer vision, and—for a moment—he wondered if he might have accidently killed himself by slashing his radial artery. If so, he'd be the first to know. He had to break free, and soon.

Thinking of nothing but saving Lee, Grant strained forward, pushing all his weight into snapping the post behind him. A slight cracking noise encouraged him. He snarled his fury, trying to conjure the same type of battle lust he might when facing a human opponent, hoping the influx of adrenaline would lend him extra strength. Another snap. Louder this time. Encouraged, Grant shoved forward again. And again. And again.

"What's going on in there, buddy?" the vampire guard asked. Soon after, he strolled back inside. "Whoa, you wolfed out on me, did you?"

Unable to respond in wolf form—and what was the point—Grant answered by putting all his strength into one more lunge. Behind him, the post finally broke, but he didn't have time to celebrate his victory. His momentum propelled him forward, where he landed snout down on the floor right at the guard's feet.

"Bravo!" The vampire snickered. Rearing back, he lifted his leg to deliver a vicious kick to Grant's side. His fur and extra body weight absorbed most of the blow, but the vampire kept doling out blow after blow until he managed to flip Grant on his back. Leering, the full length of his sharp teeth dimpling his lower lip, he said, "Naughty dog. Should have behaved."

Grant snarled.

"*Tsk tsk*. The manners of a dog."

"The same could be said of you."

Both Grant and the guard startled at the newcomer's voice.

"Who are you?" the guard asked him.

Tattoo smiled. "Marcus."

Great. Just wonderful. Grant heaved a sigh and almost wished to be back in the grips of his former predicament rather than facing the possibility of once again being saved by Marcus, aka Tattoo. Chipper as always, he strutted forward with his hands raised at the level of his head, which he'd tilted to the side as if to say, *We're cool. I'm no threat.*

"Well, Marcus, this isn't a great time," the vampire guard said. "In case you hadn't noticed."

"Yeah, you two have some weird kink thing going on?"

The guard shrugged. "Sure, tell yourself that if it'll help you see your way out the door and far away from here."

Marcus smiled again. "You're not from this clan, are you? What's your name?"

"Nope, not from this clan," the guard confirmed, not giving his name.

"So, you don't know who I am?"

"No idea. Were you the asshole making the noise outside?"

Marcus nodded.

"You're good at hiding—I'll give you that. And I'm sure you're really important in this clan, but you're no one to me. Now scram."

The guard waved him off. During the odd conversation, Grant had done his best to heal the wounds at his wrists. Although the cuts stung like a motherfucker and the ominous amount of blood matted in his fur worried him, he didn't feel dizzy and the pain had subsided. Those two things encapsulated the upside to the current situation. The various downsides, namely not knowing Marcus's motivations, nettled Grant's already taxed nerves.

Marcus, ignoring the guard's warning growl, continued to walk forward. Hands still raised at the level of his head, he acted as though the whole tenor of their conversation had remained friendly and the three of them were friends caught in the middle of some gross and unfortunate misunderstanding.

"Well," Marcus said. "I suggest you back away from my good friend here. He and I have matters to discuss."

The guard snorted. "You don't know who you're messing with. You need to back away, all the way out the fucking door. Seriously, piss off. Beat it. Vamoose."

In a bid to be the most condescending prick imaginable, the guard waved his fingers in front of Marcus's face and blew a puff of air at him. Marcus smirked when the man's breath stirred the wisps of hair that lay charmingly across his forehead. His grin widened.

"Now, now," Marcus said, waving his finger back and forth. "You're starting to irk me."

"Consider me already irked."

The two vampires, now chest to chest, raised their lips and snarled.

At least their constant posturing had secured Grant more time to heal and assess the situation on his own. Against two vampires, especially one as powerful as Marcus, he'd end up skinned alive if he dared to attack them outright. Best to play it smart and wait for them to become wrapped up and distracted by their little quarrel. As it was, Marcus kept constant vigil on Grant's whereabouts, winking when their eyes met.

"Last chance to beat it," the guard told him. "Otherwise, things will get ugly."

"Don't be silly. You've been ugly this whole time."

The guard, his eyes hard as flint, gave Marcus's bravado an unamused chuckle. "Okay, then. Here we go."

Chapter Thirty-Six

The moment the vampires leapt for each other, Grant shifted to his quadruped wolf form and lumbered on unsteady feet toward the door, toward freedom and the cool embrace of the outdoors, which would soothe his hot skin and ease the sting of his wounds. Weak at the knees and with a faltering, lopsided gait, he staggered more than he ran. His footprints appeared to belong to a werewolf who'd only just left a New Years party and would most certainly fail a field-sobriety test.

Blood loss drained him of energy. After he found Lee, he'd have to find time to fully heal to be any use in a fight. Problem was, his friend might already be captured. Grant pushed that troubling thought from his mind. He'd get there in time. He had to.

Behind him, Marcus shouted, "Super not cool, Grant."

The tone of Marcus's voice—the outrage of real betrayal—stopped Grant in his tracks. He'd assumed, perhaps unfairly, that the eccentric vampire was hostile and that whatever had brought him there would be bad news. There was a chance, however slight, that he'd been too hasty. If so, abandoning the fight would be an unforgivable act of cowardice.

Grant teetered on his feet. Woozy yet determined to do the right thing, he turned and lumbered toward the building where he'd been held captive. As he moved, he swore his very bones, grinding against each other, creaked in protest. Snow, a fine light powder in the freezing air, blew back up in his face. Vacations sucked, Grant decided. He'd work every day for the rest of his life.

Crouching low, wary of dashing in without knowing the lay of the land, Grant slunk back into the building, keeping his footsteps light and his eyes fixed on the scene in front of him.

Oblivious to anything except their own battle, the two vampires—teeth bared, eyes yellow, hair standing on end like they had a bit of feral dog in them too—swiped their claws and growled. As far as Grant could tell, they hadn't done much other than posture since he'd left. Neither of them were bloodied, not so much as a scratch. Vampires: all teeth and drama but no bite.

Marcus, who must have heard him come in, faced Grant. Suddenly, his snarl morphed into a grin. "Oh, you did come back! Good for you. And thanks."

The vampire who'd been Grant's guard took advantage of the distraction. Rearing back, he coiled to strike. Then, he did. For a moment, the world seemed to still into a snapshot of a moment. The vampire's body appeared more like a thumb smudge in a painting than a real thing: he moved that fast.

He hit Marcus full force in the stomach, who, with an *oof* and a whole arsenal of swear words spilling from his mouth, crashed into the wall and then toppled to the floor in a heap. The guard didn't give him so much as a moment to recover before he pounced—claws raised and positioned to strike.

Heedless of the danger, Grant charged forward to join the fray. Vampires, while they were physically stronger than werewolves, were susceptible to bites from other supernatural creatures. His teeth couldn't kill the monster, unless he got lucky with a deep throat bite, but he could certainly give his ex jailor a few stitches to think about.

"Shoo!" His guard kicked out at him. "Go back outside, doggie."

Snarling at the condescension, Grant made it a point to nip the delicate tendons near the heel. One good chomp on those and the mouthy fool would fold to the ground, limp and useless as wet laundry. First, though, Grant needed an opportunity to strike.

As if sensing his need, and to once again prove Lee's point that vampires are bitches, Marcus kicked the guard right in his balls. Perhaps Grant had a bit of bitch in him too. While the guard was distracted with the pain, his eyes even squeezed shut, Grant clamped down on the back of his heel and shook with all his strength. As predicted, he fell to the floor with a thump and a shrill cry.

"Nice!" Marcus said, congratulating both himself and Grant. He held his hand up for a high five, but looked down at Grant—still in wolf form—and slapped his own hand. "Go team."

The guard rolled around on the floor. Cursing them both, he said, "Once Reggie gets here, you two will regret ever crossing me. You're dead. And it'll be painful."

Marcus gave the bravado a small smile. Then, with a little shrug, he set about searching the area. For what? Grant didn't care to guess and couldn't risk turning human to ask, so he drew his lips back from his teeth and stood vigil over their captive. Each time the injured vampire tried to move, Grant pressed his muzzle closer to his neck, snarling and snapping to make his point clear: don't move.

"Ah, ha. Here we go," Marcus said.

Grant didn't risk turning his head to see what Marcus was up to now. As his plodding footsteps came nearer, Grant, uncertain what the erratic vampire might do, became increasingly uneasy. His instincts proved to be true. Marcus, holding a wooden stake that that he'd pulled from the wreckage of the post Grant had been tied to, reappeared. This time, his big grin held more malice than playful mischief.

Grant shifted back to human. "You *can't* kill him."

Ignoring him, Marcus raised the makeshift wooden stake above his head.

"Stop," Grant called. "This is murder."

Marcus rolled his eyes as if Grant were recalling some precious chestnut of a story he simply didn't have time for. "You're *so* boring. A perfect fit for our Lee."

"Thanks. Also, I'm going to ask you again to put down your weapon. We can't be on the same side if you kill him."

Groaning, while rolling his eyes—the drama queen version of patting your stomach while rubbing your head, Grant supposed—Marcus tossed the stake to the ground, where it fell and rolled with a clatter. The guard eyed the discarded weapon. His fingers twitched with clear intent.

"Pick it up," Marcus encouraged him. "Pretty please."

Grant kicked it out of his former guard's reach. "Don't. Surrender yourself; allow me to arrest you."

"That's boring. Come on, Grant. This guy wants to kill your precious Lee. Don't you want to end his days before he touches a hair on your sweet angel's head?"

"I want to follow the law," Grant snarled back. "As should you."

The injured vampire's eyes flickered from Grant's face to Marcus's, gauging whose sensibilities would win if he chose to attack again. He must have realized Grant was no match for Marcus. He let his body go limp and raised his hands upward. Sighing in disappointment, Marcus grabbed a pair of cuffs, designed for supernatural criminals, from his back pocket.

"Who are you?" Grant asked, raising his eyebrow. He'd only seen such specialized cuffs a few times.

"Well, you should have some idea. You know I consult for the police and that I'm powerful enough to remove strong enchantments. What do those two things tell you, Porter? Care to make a guess?"

The name of the organization, a specialized group that handled the highest supernatural cases, was on the tip of Grant's tongue, but he swallowed it along with a sudden wave of panic. He'd behaved honorably, according to protocol, from what he remembered. Everything he'd been told about the organization suggested that its agents played strictly by the rules—no exceptions. Marcus had skated the line here, but he'd never crossed it. And he said he'd been *testing* Grant.

"Come on," Marcus goaded him. "You know."

"The Silent Crew."

Marcus held his finger to his pursed lips, which curled in another smile, and said, "Shhh."

Chapter Thirty-Seven

Grant stood a little straighter under Marcus's intense, measuring scrutiny. Being so rigorously evaluated reminded Grant of being fresh out of the academy, except he was naked, and he'd nearly abandoned an officer to die in battle. What he wouldn't give to at least have a freshly polished pair of glossy black shoes and a crisp uniform instead of only his dick and the vague sense of impending doom.

Marcus smirked. "You can relax, Porter. I won't tell another soul about how you've spent most of your vacation covering your cock with your hand and missing obvious clues."

"That...that would be kind of you."

"On one condition."

Almost forgetting himself and the changing power dynamic, Grant stifled a growl. Repressing his irritation, he said, "What would you have me do, sir?"

Marcus smirked. "Loosen up, for starters."

"I will endeavor—"

Marcus burst out laughing, cutting Grant off. "If you're going to *endeavor* to loosen up, I suggest you start at the sentence level. But, seriously, take another vacation." Grant started to interject, but Marcus held his hand to stop him. "Then, afterward, consider a change in career."

Grant swallowed down the lump in his throat. Ever since childhood, he'd known the call of service to others. He'd thought he'd found his place when he became a cop, but his starry-eyed belief that officers were servants of the law was shattered, leaving him grasping for a new purpose. Then, he'd found a new calling when he became a PI and community advocate. Giving it up would be abandoning the part of himself who'd made an extended pack out of the people he served. But he could understand why Marcus wasn't impressed with him and why he thought Grant was unsuited for the job; he'd been running around like a mad man.

Grant said, "I know I didn't show you the best of myself, but—"

"But you have shown yourself to be loyal, honorable, and true to the law. That's exactly the type of guy the Silent Crew seeks to recruit. I've put you through your paces, and you, almost with no hitches, came through. I mean, I was a tad miffed when you dropped the trail of the vampire to chase after that bunny for Lee—" Marcus stopped to give him an indulgent smile, which he paired with an arched brow. "—But I suppose you only thought of your mark as an irritation rather than a true threat. And love, ah love, makes fools of us all as the saying goes."

"So you actually have been testing me...instead of stalking me?"

"Guilty of a little of both, I suppose."

Torn between wanting to hug Marcus or bite his ankles, Grant stood perfectly still and let himself absorb the impact of the news. Him, an ex-cop driven from the force, a member of the Silent Crew, an elite vampire organization that investigated the most dangerous supernatural criminals? It was far too good to be true. And quite likely impossible.

"I thought the Silent Crew was vampire only?" Grant said.

Marcus's facial muscles twitched. "Typically so, but we're looking to expand; this current investigation is an example of why. We're in need of a werewolf tracker. Think about it, and talk to Lee."

"Yes, I will. I—"

Marcus cut him off again. "Sorry to keep talking over you, but time is an issue. The vampire you've been hunting is dangerous. I need you to help me unmask him and then to catch him. Even if you don't wish to join our ranks, I trust you'll do this out of duty?"

"Of course," Grant nodded. "But how do you know my guy is your guy?"

Marcus tapped his nose. When Grant drew back in surprise, he said, "I know it's not typical for us vampires to hunt by smell, but our guy uses the same trick wherever he goes. He masks his scent with Coppertone and Old Spice, or some other dreadful, overpowering combination, and works an enchantment that fully blocks vampire vision. Werewolves are immune—at least the effects of his spell are not as severe."

Grant thought back to the blurry white outline of the guy who'd bound him and how the image shimmered as though he were looking at the vampire's face through water. Such magic, far beyond anything he'd encountered, would make for a powerful foe indeed. Overcome with a sudden wave of dread, Grant stammered, "What has this guy done? He seems to have some type of personal issue with Lee."

Pursing his lips, Marcus cocked his head to the side as if to say, *Well, that isn't good.*

"Please tell me," Grant said, his voice shaking.

Relenting, Marcus said, "He kills other vampires. As of now, we're unclear on his motive. All we know is that he picks powerful vampires, real up-and-comers in their clans, and somehow lures them away to meet the sun. He's killed at least a dozen in the last year that way."

Without hearing another word, Grant shifted back to wolf and dashed toward the hotel. Lungs burning, his legs and feet feeling like four stiff wooden logs beneath him, Grant forced himself to maintain a constant, loping run until the pain almost surpassed endurance. By the time the shadow of the hotel materialized, spilling like ink on the white snow, his chest burned and an ominous blackness crept into the corners of his vision. Still, he pressed forward.

"Stop!" Marcus thundered down in front of him, landing with a whoosh of air and flinging snow into Grant's face. Eyes blazing, he said, "Making dumb decisions doesn't help Lee. I know this is a matter of love for you, so let me be the brains right now."

Grant shook the snow off his head, using his paws to wipe it from his eyes. Briefly, he thought about defying Marcus's order. Lee—his precious Lee—needed him now and he'd already wasted too much time sorting out the details of Marcus's strange behavior and background.

"Grant," Marcus continued. "I know you love him, and I do too"—Marcus raised his eyebrow at Grant's slight, rumbling growl—"as a *friend*. But we need to stay clear-headed. We can't run into the fray without a solid game plan."

Although the blood in his veins, under direct order from his frantic heart, pumped furiously through him, Grant remained wise enough to concede the point. Getting captured—or killed—didn't help anyone, especially not Lee. Feeling foolish yet again, he nodded to let Marcus know he was listening.

"Good, glad you came to your senses. This is a dangerous foe, my friend. Not someone you want to chase after half-cocked."

Grant gave the stern warning another nod to let Marcus know he understood the risks. Patiently, he waited for the vampire to resume. Hopefully, he had some type of plan already in the works that Grant, addled by his fear for Lee's safety, could cosign.

"Shift," Marcus commanded him.

Grant did as ordered. Totally naked, he stood in the snow and waited for Marcus, who'd miraculously transformed into a serious down-to-business member of an elite kill squad, to give further instruction. He considered Grant with steely eyes, as if trying to gauge how much of a liability he'd be. Under the vampire's scrutiny, Grant wordlessly bore the stinging cold of the wind at his back, the snow at his feet. He'd die before he so much as flinched.

Marcus gave his show of grit a slight smile. "So, there's a ball tonight. Grab Lee and put on your dancing shoes."

Chapter Thirty-Eight

The moment Lee, unharmed yet perturbed, opened the door, Grant let out a grand whoosh of air. Hand clutching his heart, he sagged against the wall and then eventually collapsed into a hyperventilating lump on the floor. By now, he expected the mischief-maker to have already made his move. Grant's imagination conjured endless images of Lee being tortured before being sent off to die in the sun, his sweet smile twisted in agony and his perfect, smooth skin—so kissably soft—splitting and tearing like an overripe tomato.

Tilting his eyebrow at Grant's melodrama, Lee grunted. "Good lord, what happened to your clothes *this* time?"

Grant ignored the question. Still breathing hard, he said, "You're safe. Thank God you're safe."

"Why wouldn't I be?"

Explanations dried on Grant's lips. He stood so suddenly that Lee, surprised by the quickness of his advance, bumped against the wall, splaying his hand behind to steady himself and to keep from falling. Wide-eyed, aroused or startled, he studied Grant's heaving sides and his tangled mass of black hair that, no matter how hard Grant tried, wouldn't soothe back down into something resembling order. He hoped his disheveled state appealed to Lee, that he, like Grant, wanted to ride out the wild streak until the two reduced themselves to base animals.

"Good lord, what happened to you?" Lee asked.

"Explain later. Kiss me. Now."

"Excuse me?"

Grant slipped one arm around Lee, using it to tug their bodies tightly together. Gazing down into Lee's shifting eyes, a swirl of black and so much forest green that there was a bite of pine in the air, Grant conveyed his desires by pressing his erection against Lee's. He longed for total surrender but would settle for a fifty-fifty split.

"My, my, my," Lee breathed. "Bring me the torture rack that brought you to this state."

"Kiss me," Grant said again.

"Oh, Mr. In Charge. We'll see. We'll see."

Defiantly, Lee licked his lips enough to make them glisten invitingly in the soft light, but kept his distance as he ran one hand up the length of Grant's body, using the other to massage Grant's cock. Lee chuckled at Grant's frustrated moan and outright laughed when Grant bent to caress the crook of his neck, begging Lee to end his torment but, at the same time, wanting that sweet, sharp edge between fire and flood to last forever.

"Lee," Grant breathed against Lee's neck, gingerly nipping at his Adam's apple. "I love you so much. I—"

As Lee pulled away, his body stiff and unresponsive, Grant realized his mistake. Well, the mistake he'd made other than pawing at his lover in a hallway, where at least one passerby had taken note and given them a long whistle and a mocking hubba-hubba. He'd been slightly embarrassed at the time, not enough to quit, but not half as mortified as he was now.

"Lee... I..."

Through narrowed eyes, he said, "You...what, were you lying...about what you just said?"

Grant swallowed down a wave of panic that threatened to send him bolting down the hallway, his hands waving frantically as he fled. This was worse than his snafu with David. At least he'd baked him cupcakes and attempted traditional romance before the love train became horribly derailed. Right now, masks were falling from the ceiling, and oh shit, he was on a crashing plane. A moment longer and he'd be in a car, then a boat, then he'd have exhausted all types of transportation and he'd burn and crash walking to his doom.

"Freaking out over there are we, dear heart?"

Yes. Trying to buy some time and to sound fully in control, Grant said, "Let's go inside. I don't want to have this conversation here."

Much to Grant's relief, Lee went without protest, ducking his head to hide his features behind a beautiful halo of hair before Grant retrieved a proper read of his expression. For all he knew, Lee would be spitting mad and ready to box; the click of the door would be the ding of the bell and the fight would begin.

"Grant?"

"Y—yes?"

"Stop worrying so much. Come over here and talk to me."

Lee patted the patch of bed beside him. Under his slight weight, the mattress hardly buckled. When Grant sat, Lee slumped against his shoulder. Instead of drawing back, he allowed Grant's body to prop him upright. His fingers lazily trailed Grant's leg, stopping short of his upper thigh. More teasing. God, Grant loved the teasing. He'd miss that the most.

"So—" Lee began. "Let's pretend the hallway didn't happen. Just more of Fluff monster's bad timing, that's all."

Grant's heart pulled out its violin and prepared to play the saddest sad-sack song it knew, something dour enough to make children holding puppies cry. "I understand. We broke the rules earlier, but that was different. Now we—"

"Stop. Stop right there."

"I'm sorry—"

Lee gave his leg a light pinch. "Fluff monster, stop talking and kiss me."

"What?"

"You win, dear heart. I want you to kiss me. And, honestly, I'm the one who's supposed to need an invitation."

Grant, not wanting to spit in the face of fate by delaying, forced Lee onto his back. Greedily, he pressed their lips together but slowed the pace to a crawl the second Lee tried to have his own slip-of-the-tongue moment. Lee's low moan of frustration when Grant cut off his path vibrated in Grant's mouth, and he tasted the tang of salt and the sweet punch of Lee himself. Grant drank it in, loving the contrast and the way Lee tangled his fingers in his hair, pulling gently and then sharply to steer Grant's mouth where he wanted it.

"My cock," Lee whispered.

Grant tore his mouth away from Lee's with effort and trailed a series of hot kisses down the length of his slender body, stopping to lick and nip the tender nooks and crannies as he stripped Lee of his clothes. Lee continued to push Grant's head downward, begging and breathing in the span of one heartbeat until Grant finally kissed the first curl at Lee's abdomen.

"Come on," Lee said. "Come on."

Instead of submitting to Lee's demands, Grant nuzzled the sensitive flesh around Lee's belly button. Lee's long fingers twined in Grant's hair. After yanking Grant to his cock, Lee pressed the tip of it against Grant's lips. Still playing it coy, Grant licked the head—once, twice, three times—and enjoyed how the spritely thing bobbled back to his mouth each time.

"How's my timing now?" Grant asked when Lee grunted.

"You...you *are* a monster. All who came before me were right."

Grant chuckled at Lee's ire but finally gave in and took Lee's whole cock into his mouth, right down to the last inch. Gasping in pleasure, Lee lifted himself in time with the rise and fall of Grant's head as he glided his mouth along the velvet flesh of Lee's shaft. Grant listened to the hitches in Lee's breathing as they changed to rapid gasps. Grant broke away, panting.

"Lee," Grant said. "Lee."

"Yes. If you're asking to be inside me, the answer is yes."

Lee's little airy clucks of pleasure continued as Grant massaged his asshole with lubricant. Those generous satisfied murmurs combined with Lee's occasional punctuated moans were almost enough to tip Grant over the edge. Their pleasure, as well as their lives, entwined and neither thread would easily separate no matter how hard life pulled. That's what Grant wanted. That's the future he had to communicate with his body because he obviously wasn't getting there with words or cupcakes.

"Come on," Lee urged him. Emphasizing his need, he wrapped his legs around Grant's torso to pull him closer. "Please."

Helpless to resist such pleading, Grant used one leg to prop open Lee's, leaving his hole accessible to Grant's aching cock. Then, gently but assertively, he thrust inside, at the same time grabbing hold of Lee's shaft. He took a moment to relish the soft, satisfied moan Lee let loose as his body welcomed Grant's invasion and how his hard cock twitched in Grant's firm grip. Encouraged, Grant rocked himself deeper, timing the rhythm of his thrusts to the beat of his heart.

"Do you like this?" Grant asked him. "I can stop if—"

"The only thing you should stop is talking."

Grant gave the rugged order a breathy chuckle, which he tried to infuse with confidence. Instead, he ended up sounding a lot like he did with his first lover—shaky and full of childish glee.

Lee didn't notice the lie behind Grant's bravado, or if he did, he didn't care. He twisted his hands in the sheets and tore holes in the fabric with his claws, simultaneously kneading and shredding while Grant rammed himself into Lee and ran his slick hand the length of Lee's shaft. Around his temples, damp and glistening with sweat, his long chestnut hair clung and darkened to a russet brown. His mouth hung open but no words came out—just animal whines and grunts that drove Grant's heart from a frantic pitter-patter to a drumroll.

"Harder," Lee said. "Harder."

Blood pounded in Grant's ears as he struggled to fulfill the request before he lost control. He pulled almost all the way out before he surged inside Lee again, going deeper, deeper, deeper with each thrust until Lee's body shook in climax. Under Grant's hand, Lee's cock jerked; his come shot up to his chest. Grant, with a savage growl of satisfaction, did the same.

Chapter Thirty-Nine

Lee, his chestnut hair tangled and damp from sweat, rested his head against Grant's chest. Humming a chipper tune Grant recognized but couldn't identify, one of those frustrating tip-of-the-tongue brainteasers, Lee ran his finger down to Grant's navel and then to his neck. The featherlight caresses, so near a tickle, stirred another round of desire, a feeling Grant quashed before he got too far off track. The whole vampire-murderer-on-the-loose situation should have stopped him the first time, but loving Lee exposed his best and worst impulses.

Speaking of worst impulses. Grant picked a loose strand of Lee's hair. Raising it to his lips, he kissed it gently before tucking it back behind Lee's ear. "Can I say the words now, or is my timing still off?"

Perhaps it was just his imagination, but Grant swore he sensed Lee's impish smile in his words. "Say it if you mean it and want to hold me like this until death do you part."

"Ouch, low dig at my mortality."

Lee sat up. His sharp incisors protruded in wicked humor. "Still want to say the words?"

"Yes, I suppose."

All the colors of the aurora borealis danced in Lee's eyes. "Say them, then. Come on, dear heart. I've been dying to hear them."

"I love you."

"I *know*."

Lee bit his bottom lip, apparently to inhibit the huge grin that eventually broke through. Grant had never seen Lee so bubbly; his happiness was a far more dignified and mellow brandy. But here he was practically clapping his hands together like a trained seal about to receive a bucket of fish.

"Also, do you *really*?" Lee asked. "Everything about me, including my teeth?"

"Yes. And I love your fangs, especially their bite."

Holding his breath in anticipation, Grant waited for Lee to stop coyly twirling the strand of hair around his finger, wrapping it tightly the way he'd always bent Grant to his will. But God, Grant loved it. He treasured each moment Lee lured him to some madness with a sweet smile and a witty, playfully cutting remark. He wanted to follow that trail all the way back to his lush mouth, plump after their lovemaking.

"Anything to say to fluff monster?" Grant prompted.

Sudden tears pooled in Lee's eyes. His voice shaking with emotion, Lee said, "I love you. I'm sorry. I'm sorry for—"

Grant plugged Lee's apology hole with a suave kiss. When he broke away, he said, "Okay, that was everything I hoped it would be and more, and I promise to make you cupcakes and give you foot rubs later, but there's something I need to tell you..."

"Go on."

"The vamp who's been trailing us is more of a problem than either of us initially believed."

"Not him again." Lee furrowed his brow. The severe V-cut in his forehead hinted at him having a short temper on the topic of their stalker. Lee had been annoyed enough when the persistent asshole kept interrupting their brawls. Now that he inserted himself between their lovemaking, Lee might just fly off the handle and go find him on his own. Grant, no matter what, had to prevent an impromptu rogue vampire hunt. Telling Lee he'd been kidnapped wouldn't suit that end, so Grant kept that information to himself.

Letting his canines show in a way he knew Lee thought cute, Grant donned his most disarming smile. "Sweetness—"

"Oh, I'm 'sweetness' now? That was quick."

"Do you prefer 'baby cakes'?"

Lee puckered his lips and shook his head. "Noooo."

"Vampoline?"

"Only if you want me to tell you to bounce."

Although Lee's brow remained furrowed, indicating his ill humor persisted despite Grant's silly jokes, the twinkle in his eyes suggested he enjoyed their banter more than the idea of finding their tormenter and beating the crap out of him. That was something. Encouraged, Grant said, "The Silent Crew are on the case, Lee. This guy is dangerous."

"How do you know the Silent Crew are here?"

"They approached me..."

"Yes...but why?"

Shit. Lee's ability to detect Grant's lies was almost so good it could pass as supernatural. As much as Grant loved Lee's adorable overprotective streak when he was defending Grant from mean words, he didn't want the love of his life to fly off into the night to fight a vampire equally or more powerful. He needed to keep Lee safe. He could only manage that if he stuck with the plan and had the backup of the Silent Crew.

"Grant..." Lee poked him.

"Promise me something before I tell you."

"I already don't like the sound of that, so no guarantees."

"Not negotiable. If you won't promise me, I won't tell you, and you can't help me."

Lee sat back on his haunches, delivering a level, cold stare that would have run a chill down Grant's spine had he not known it wasn't for him. Lee's fangs protruded. "Who hurt you? Was it Marcus?"

"No one. But I've been dragged into a case."

Yellow now, Lee's eyes bore into his. "Grant, tell me."

"Promise me you won't do anything, first."

Lee hissed.

"Is that a 'yes' hiss or a 'no' hiss?"

"Yes hiss, I suppose."

Not quite believing Lee, but seeing no other choice but to tell him the relevant, Grant gave Lee a brief breakdown of the conversation he'd had with Marcus, leaving out the whole bit about being tied and threatened beforehand. Hopefully, with luck, Lee would never bite into that tidbit, and he'd only be slightly miffed that the Silent Crew would approach Grant for such a dangerous mission, especially when Lee apparently thought of Grant as an overpuffed fluff ball.

"And he just started talking to you about this out of the blue?"

Grant hid the lie in the truth. "He broke the enchantment the mischief-maker put on you, remember?"

Lee narrowed his eyes. "Yes. That wasn't so long ago."

"Well, then, you know how I met with Marcus."

"But then you went to talk to the other cop they dispatched. What happened with that?"

Hiding his nervous smile behind an awkward cough, Grant slid his arm around Lee and tugged their bodies together for a tight hug. Somehow, Grant hoped the touchy feelies would override Lee's natural predatory instincts, especially those that told him Grant was keeping secrets.

For added insurance, Grant kissed and licked the long line of Lee's neck. Now that he was free to use sex as a weapon, he planned on unsheathing his cock and impaling Lee on it whenever he thought of running off toward danger. He counted on that strategy to prove more effective than the begging and pleading he'd done as a friend.

Nuzzling the skin under Lee's neck, Grant breathed, "So...about our date tonight."

Eyes closed, lips parted in pleasure, Lee said, "You sure you wouldn't rather stay in, and by 'in' I mean balls deep?"

Grant chuckled. Truthfully, Lee's suggestion sounded amazing, but he committed to the plan outlined by Marcus. In order to satisfy his part of the scheme, he needed to be out in the open with Lee.

"Let's wine, dine, and dance. Do all the romantic stuff I should have done with the pretty boys you prescribed me to get over David."

Lee frowned at the reminder that the trip began with him basically telling Grant to have sex with anything that moved. The idea Lee might have actually been jealous the entire time brought a huge smile to Grant's face, which he had to repress before it became a full-on preening grin.

Lee studied Grant's face. "You're hiding something. I know it."

"You're right. I am."

Lee straightened. He flipped his hands in the air as if to say, *Go ahead, tell me, then.*

Smirking, Grant said, "You ready for the big reveal?"

"Give it to me hard. You know that's the way I like it."

Leaning over to whisper in Lee's ear, Grant confessed, "I can't dance."

Chapter Forty

Grant hadn't been exaggerating about his grossly incompetent dancing, which mostly included twisting his upper body while his lower remained stiff and stationary. He knew the effect was all wrong, not to mention comical, but he still couldn't manage to summon the courage to wiggle his hips suggestively like the vampires around him, who sashayed as though they'd crawled from their crypts with flowers clamped between their teeth—decked out and ready to tango.

Lee glared at Grant's scuffed loafers, which kept stepping on Lee's shiny black dance shoes. "I'm grateful to be undead and unable to bleed out through my feet."

"I'm trying here!"

"Trying to look like a giant bobblehead? 'Cause you're nailing it!" Lee said and gave his ass a playful pinch. "But I love your two left feet as much as the rest of you."

The nearby vampires snickered. Even over the blaring music, they heard every line of their conversation, and Grant got the sense they enjoyed the salacious gossip more than the party. No contest. Werewolves preached discretion in their relationships, preferring to keep their displays of affection firmly behind doors. Vampires, well, they stuck their noses right in his and Lee's business. Literally.

"They had sex! I smell it, guys!"

"Are you two...together now?" another asked as he and his partner swung by them.

"They have to be! They're getting married!"

Gasps rippled through the crowd. Grant, suppressing an embarrassed groan, focused on the mission rather than the delighted whoops and cheers of Lee's clan. Marcus said the mischief-maker was sure to make some type of move tonight, and he'd be desperate, hopefully to the point of carelessness, with the fete ending and Lee slipping from his grasp.

Grant searched for a sign of the signature stench of sunblock and cologne. He didn't see any blurry white faces between the gliding walls of dancers either. Each time he thought he did, a sense of dread overwhelmed him, blocking out his normally meticulous reason. The possibility Lee might find out Grant had been attacked earlier, and respond impetuously and emotionally, hung over Grant's neck like an executioner's axe.

Later, when they were in bed and Lee had been sated with some amazing sex and danger was nowhere in sight, Grant would confess. Then, maybe, he'd get a nibble of a cussing out rather than a chomp.

"You keep sniffing the air," Lee said. "It makes me believe I was right earlier and you're not telling me everything."

"No, no, no. Told you everything."

"You're a real shit liar," Lee drawled.

Grant gave the accurate observation a breezy smile, which shook and then vanished to make way for a concerned frown. Grant smoothed his brow when he realized he'd scrunched his face, a dead giveaway that his mind lingered elsewhere. Observant and perpetually worried, Lee would eventually piece together the threads of Grant's deception.

Rather than answer, Grant drew Lee close enough to build torturous heat and friction as their hips rubbed. Their hearts, so close together, chattered on like a couple of know-it-alls who'd always shipped each other and saw their love as canon all along. Sighing in contentment, Lee rested his head against Grant's chest. The smooth cascade of his hair brushed the top of Grant's hand, and their hearts beat a little faster.

"You and your heart," Lee said. "Always leading the dance."

"Yours is moving fast too, mister."

"It's dodging your feet."

Grant plastered a genuine smile on his face. Danger or not, he wanted to enjoy his night of true romance with Lee, the first of many to come if the fates were kind. But the pesky, nagging worry crept back on him: the mischief-maker would be here tonight. He'd catch wind of Grant's escape, and he'd be prepared.

"You're doing it again," Lee mumbled against his chest. "I can feel your body stiffen, not in the way that excites me."

Grant said, "I'm being vigilant after the attack. And you should be too."

"Why? I thought you said the Silent Crew were here taking care of it, and you guys concocted some plan together. That I'm *bait* for."

Grant laughed at Lee's playful indignation. "Yes, but you're such an adorable squirmy worm."

Lee lifted his head. Under the bright white lights, the blues and greens stood out, highlighted by the warmth of the chocolate-brown laced through the iris. His mouth, almost always smiling at his own secret mischief, twisted upward, a couple of sharp hooks that declared he was more predator than prey and Grant better not forget it.

Grant scrunched his nose. "You're so cute when you're thinking about something devious."

"I *know*."

They pressed their foreheads together so that their laughter shared the same sweet air. Grant, feeling inspired, brushed his lips against Lee's in a soft kiss.

Their mirth was rudely interrupted when Brian, with Cherub hanging in his arms, swirled nearby. Snickering in a way that conveyed no mirth or warmth, he said, "I always knew you were fucking him behind my back. And here you are offering proof. Good to see it all out in the open at last." Brian aimed his glare at Grant. "Congrats on taming this one. You should know you'll never be the most important thing in his life. Fangs first, that's him."

No longer hiding his distaste or revulsion with Lee's ex, Grant said, "I'd ask him to live for me but never to die. Your request was pure narcissism, and I'm glad Lee refused it. Now bounce."

One of Lee's clan, hovering nearby, asked, "Did Noodle just use slang?"

An appreciative, if somewhat strained, chuckle circulated through the gathered crowd, growing louder toward the end. Trying to capitalize on the break in the tension, Lee said, "Don't be too impressed, guys. He learned it about an hour ago."

"Guilty," Grant confessed. "Lee tells me I'm going to need to read the Urban Dictionary every day to hang with you guys."

"Probably twice a day," a grinning vampire quipped. "And you'll need a tutor."

Embarrassed but pleased to be part of the clan rather than outside it—despite their stark differences, Lee's family had grown on him—Grant didn't bother to hide the flush in his face or the laughter in his voice when he said, "I was hoping for private lessons."

Brian's already stamped-on smile grew sharper around the edges. There was malice in it that went beyond sour grapes or mere jealousy and tripped Grant's alarm bells. Although they were searching for a vampire, one who reeked of sunblock and cologne, Grant detected the energy he'd felt at each crime scene wafting from the pair in front of them. Somehow, they were involved. Using his body, Grant blocked their path to Lee.

"What's wrong?" Cherub asked, his big eyes round and innocent.

"Nothing at all," Grant assured them, but he pressed the button to alert the standby members of the Silent Crew.

"What did you just do?" Brian asked. Eyes narrowed, nostrils flaring, he stared Grant down with the intensity of a bull about to charge the matador.

Lee, being his protective self, tried to wriggle out from behind Grant to stand out in front, a barrier between any danger. Sometimes their similarities vexed Grant— now, for instance. He needed Lee, the target of the killer, to be vigilant instead of exposed, sensible instead of brave, alive instead of dead. Trying to be gentle, Grant grabbed hold of Lee's arm and dragged him backward out of the fray. Of course he didn't cooperate. Seconds later, he was right back—hackles up, teeth out, and eyes bright yellow.

"Hey, guys, let's keep things breezy," one of Lee's clan said. Her voice was tense to the point of snapping. "No use in fighting on the last night of the party, huh?"

"I don't want trouble," Grant said. "More than happy to call it here."

"Oh, you're just so proud and noble," Brian sneered. "Everyone's favorite corked-fang werewolf. No wonder Lee loves you so much."

Looking, for once, like something other than a simpering fool, Cherub twisted his pert mouth in an angry knot. Grant followed the line of his hard stare directly to Lee, who, oblivious to the other vampire's growing hostility, focused all his attention on Brian. Cherub reached out his hand to grab hold of Brian. Pouting, he said, "You said you were over him. I was the only one for you."

Brian brushed him off. When he lifted Cherub's arm from his, the laced sleeve of Cherub's frilly overcoat lifted, exposing the red flesh beneath, scrubbed to the point the skin was raw. Grant wondered what the seemingly innocent vampire had worked so vigorously to remove that he'd nearly rubbed off a patch of his own arm. Mindful of the danger but not caring, he bent to sniff the vampire's skin. Faint but present, the tinge of sunblock and cheap cologne.

Chapter Forty-One

No one moved. The tiny hairs on the back of Grant's neck stood on end. An anticipatory tingle ran down his spine, alerting his inner wolf to the dangers ahead. It listened. Fangs—heavy on his bottom lip—inched ever downward until they grazed the first bit of skin. Grant lapped the droplets of blood, practically daring Cherub, their mischief-maker unmasked, to see him as food. Driving him to frenzy was a risky proposition. Bloodlust often made vampires weaker, prone to stupid mistakes, but it most certainly made them more vicious.

"Grant, *move* back," Lee warned Grant, his grip tightening. "This fight is ours—mine and my clan's. Please, Grant."

Grant ignored Lee's pleadings and stationed himself between the vampire who wanted to rip out his heart and the vampire who already had it in his palm. Someday, hopefully, the Silent Crew would jump into the fray, saving them both. Until then, Grant planted himself firmly in the middle as a buffer.

"Grant," Lee growled. "You're no match. Move it."

"Listen to your sweetie pie," Cherub said.

"No chance," Grant responded.

Brian, who'd grown far more cautious as the situation escalated, finally stepped up to stand next to Cherub. Fidgeting, he ran his hands over his goose-bump-speckled arms, which had turned the same chalky white as his face.

His gaze darted side to side. In a trembling voice, he said, "Lee's nothing compared to you, baby. No need to fight to prove it. Let's leave this shit party. Go get your fangs yanked and live life as mortals, just like we planned."

"I tested you. Like the rest, you failed," Cherub said. "All I wanted was to be number one in someone's heart."

Lee snorted at the earnest declaration.

Cherub morphed. The sweet innocence melted away bit by bit until a sharp-toothed, yellow-eyed monster stood in its place, all spittle and frazzled hair and sharp, jaundiced claws licking the air in anticipation of carving into flesh. Maybe it was his imagination, but Grant swore a tinge of red lurked in the dark black pupils of his eyes.

Brian placed his hand on Cherub's shoulder. "Baby...come on..."

In a blur of motion, Cherub snapped his hand backward, hitting Brian directly in the face. The man, nothing more than a fragile human with the bones of a bird, collapsed on the floor in a heap. The smell of blood, as old as a penny in a grandpa's pocket, saturated the air. Grant didn't risk looking down at the wreckage. Assuming Brian was most likely dead, he focused on calming Cherub and prayed Lee would keep a lid on his own boiling temper in the meantime.

"Hey," Grant said in a conciliatory tone. "I understand why you're upset. I get passed up all the time too. That was actually the reason for this vacation. My ex boyfriend dumped me and then posted a whole slew of lies online."

Cherub snorted. "I bet you don't even know my real name."

Yikes. Grant licked his lip and tried to think whether or not the taciturn vampire had ever actually supplied his real name. Calling him Cherub hit the wrong notes if he aimed to deescalate the situation, and he didn't want to end like Brian, dead or deadish on the floor.

"It's Reggie," Lee said, stepping forward. "You've been in this clan for a little under a year. We played badminton once. You beat me."

"You play badminton?" Grant asked.

Studying Grant through the narrowed yellow slits of his eyes, Reggie said, "Well, *obviously*."

Lee smirked. "Yeah, Grant. Dumb question. Werewolves, am I right?"

At first, Grant considered shushing Lee, whose method of conflict resolution usually consisted of a back rub or a good cussing out—two ends of a rather stark in-or-out-of-his-graces spectrum. But then the genius of it dawned on Grant. Nothing got vampires talking like old rivalries and werewolves verses vampires was as old as it got.

Reggie bared his teeth at Grant. "Piss off. Go howl at the moon or something."

By his own magic, Lee's smirk managed to double as a leer. "Yeah, go howl at the moon."

Lifting his nose in disdain, Lee regarded Grant as though he were little more than a stray dog that reeked of trash and humped legs. The act was so convincing that Grant momentarily forgot his role in the pageant and stared at Lee with what he hoped were hurt puppy-dog eyes. A sharp pinch on his ass reminded him he had an image to maintain, lines to say, vampires to affront.

Playing along, Grant said, "That's rich coming from a couple of fat ticks."

Both vampires bristled at the insult. Reggie turned to Lee. "You fuck this walking flea circus?"

"What can I say? He knows how to bury his bone in my back yard and can do a satisfactory number of tricks."

Reggie sneered. "Not sit and stay, apparently. Your dog should have stayed tethered to his post."

Lee's body stiffened. *Shit. Shit. Shit.* Before Grant had a chance to mutter so much as a *don't even think about it,* Lee had gone from sexy brooding vampire to sexy brutal killing machine. Claws extended and hissing like a provoked cat, he lunged at Reggie, knocking the smaller vampire to the floor. They struggled for dominance—a blur of limbs, teeth, and beautiful chestnut hair—while Grant searched for some way to get Lee to a safe place, far far away from the sun.

Where the hell was his backup? For a group as exalted as the Silent Crew, they certainly took their sweet time responding to calls. And he needed them here. A werewolf was no match for a vampire in a one-on-one tussle. But Grant had no option but to engage.

Grant shifted to withstand the blows. Acting on instinct, he untangled who was who in the knot of limbs and flashing teeth by smell, separating Lee by the dash of fresh rain that followed him like a shadow. When an opportunity presented itself, he sunk his teeth into Reggie's calf and dragged him across the floor, flinging him as far away as the slick marble would carry him. Annoyed by the unwelcome intervention, Lee sputtered and tossed his hands into the air as though he couldn't believe Grant would be so foolish.

Sorry, Lee. I'm not going to let you get yourself killed.

Saving his own life, on the other hand, might have been another matter.

Reggie recovered quickly. In a flash, he sprang to his feet and whooshed on an angry gust directly toward Grant. Fueled by anger and already much stronger and faster, he cut a line through the crowd of vampires who had gathered to block his path, knocking them over and scattering them like bowling pins.

Grant, who'd backed himself back against a wall, dove to the side right as Reggie's claws sliced upward in a deadly arch. Carried by his own forward momentum, the enraged vampire slammed into the wall. Cracks shot up around the impact site going as far as the ceiling. Bits of plaster, heavy chunks of it along with a loose white powder, rained down on his head.

"Get out of here, Grant!" Lee shouted. "We've got this."

Yeah, no. Grant understood his own limitations in a fight against a powerful vampire, but he also knew Lee's clan to be a group of mostly peaceful professionals—bankers, lawyers, teachers—and he couldn't abandon them in good conscience.

Grant shook his head in response.

Twisting his mouth in frustration, Lee stalked toward Grant, looking for all the world like an angry librarian about to chew out a disruptive teen. He didn't get very far. Reggie, once again on his feet and ready to fight, intercepted his path. Grabbing hold of Lee's collar, he flew to the ceiling and then out the window.

Chapter Forty-Two

The night sky, overflowing with stars, reminded Grant that dawn loomed around the curved horizon. The sun wouldn't rise for at least another two hours. Reggie, traveling faster by air, would cover ground quickly, easily putting miles between them. On top of that, he'd knocked Lee out cold once before with a powerful enchantment, and he was likely to do so again. Grant's heart beat faster the longer he thought about the odds, but he didn't have time to dwell on his panic and fear. Lee needed saving.

Grant shifted back to his human form to ask, "Can anyone carry me?"

At that moment, the doors to the ballroom flung open. Marcus, flanked by two other vampires, rushed into the room. The harsh words Grant planned to shout died on his lips when he evaluated Marcus's condition. Cracked and bleeding, his lips drew back over blood-coated canines and his cheeks and neck were spattered with bruises that floated like clouds on his pale skin. One of his pant legs was torn up the center.

"Get some pants and hop on," Marcus yelled at Grant. "We need you to track."

One of Lee's clan, whose version of dressed up was a designer track suit that probably cost five weeks of pay, kindly stripped off his clothes and tossed them at Grant. "Find that fucker," he said. "Bring back our Lee."

Grant nodded and said, "Thanks. I will."

Not wasting any more time, Grant wrapped his arms and legs tightly around Marcus. "North," Grant told him. "Hurry, the trail will fade fast."

Marcus leapt upward. Grant's stomach lurched at the speed of their ascent; Grant swore the damn thing rose so high it knocked on his tonsils as if to say, "Hey, remember what we had for lunch?" Fighting off the nausea, Grant clung to Marcus, wincing in sympathy when the vampire groaned in pain as Grant's heels dug into his sides.

Air whipped the clothes around their bodies, drowning out the shouts and orders of the vampires who flew beside them. Grant, with the aid of his wolf, heard most of their chatter, but even to his sharp ears, a lot of words sounded like gobbledygook. Matters weren't helped by the fact they used a lot of jargon Grant assumed was specific to the Silent Crew.

"Keep going this direction," Grant shouted to Marcus after taking a deep whiff of air, the cold of it burning his nostrils. "That's where the scent is strongest."

"Affirmative," Marcus shouted back. The other two nodded.

Up ahead, Grant swore a flickering light, reminiscent of the way Lee always tilted his cell phone's flashlight directly into Grant's eye whenever he tried to sneak outside to smoke, flashed in the distance. Accidentally, of course. Grant couldn't complain too much. Lee's strategy had cured him of the nasty habit.

"Do you see that?" Grant asked Marcus. "The blinking to our left?"

Marcus swiveled his head to look in the direction Grant indicated. After a long, thoughtful pause, he said, "Yeah, I see it. Pursue or stay on course?"

The light scent of sunblock and cologne smelled the strongest going in the opposite direction of the odd flashing light, but with the wind twirling the scents haphazardly, Grant decided to trust his gut instincts over his sniffer. Smart and resourceful, Lee was the type to improvise; he wouldn't go to his grave a quivering chump. Not only would he not go gently into the good night, he'd rage about the dying of his cell phone battery.

"I think the light is a signal from Lee. Alter course."

When Marcus tilted his body to go in the opposite direction, Grant slid off his back and dangled at an awkward angle with his own legs over his head. Grant stared into the pitch black nighttime landscape, imagining himself falling until the vague shadowy shapes became hard points of light. Acting quickly to steady himself, Grant wrapped his fists in the remains of Marcus's frilly silk shirt. The delicate silk tore instantly under the strain of his weight.

"Grab him," Marcus ordered.

One of the other vampires looped his arms around Grant's torso and heaved him back on top of Marcus.

"Thanks!" Grant shouted.

The vampire, starkly different from Marcus with his crew cut and pressed uniform that smelled of starch and the heat from an iron, nodded. He lifted his thin lips in a smile so narrow it almost vanished into his square chin. Grant waved back, trying to put as much pep into it as he could muster under the circumstances.

"Do you still see the light?" Marcus asked.

Grant pointed. "Yes. There."

"Hold on tighter this time!" Marcus said. This time, he gave Grant a five count before sharply descending. Cold air nipped at Grant's flesh, cutting through the expensive tracksuit as though it were nothing but thin sheets of toilet paper. He wish he hadn't ripped up the evening clothes he'd worn to look spiffy for Lee's viewing pleasure. In retrospect, he should have dressed for battle instead of a ball—sticking to baggy clothing that would allow him to shift to wolf with ease—but he couldn't go back in time to make practical decisions.

They landed with a heavy thud. Powdery snow shot up under Marcus's feet, covering another pair of fresh footprints. Grant immediately shifted to wolf to find the trail.

"Is it our guy?" Marcus asked.

Grant nodded.

"Awesome. Let us lead the way. Stay in back in case things get..."

As best as he could as a wolf, Grant cocked his eyebrow.

"Right," Marcus grinned. "You're already hairy."

As instructed, Grant trailed behind the trio of vampires, occasionally stopping to sniff to make sure they were still on the right path. He didn't understand why Reggie had chosen to travel on the ground, but he didn't trust how easy it had become to track him. Nothing about the situation sat easily on Grant's shoulders.

"Be alert," Marcus said. "Something's off."

The other two vampires nodded in agreement. They rolled their shoulders and hunkered down into a defensive position—one hand on their holstered guns, the other held out in front of them as if to ward off a blow. Their lips moved in time. Chanting, Grant realized. With any luck, the incantations would prevent a powerful enchantment from snaring them.

Unable to work any magic himself, Grant relied on the three vampires to protect him. In other circumstances, being so helpless might have bothered him. But Grant could only focus on one thing: Lee. His heart. His friend. His life. And he was right in front of him.

"Grant," Lee said through cracked lips. "Run."

Chapter Forty-Three

Although Lee delivered the plea using his never-fail-to-get-what-I-want voice, combined with a wide-eyed simper, Grant refused to so much as budge. Lee was crazy if he thought Grant would run off and leave him in the custody of a murderous vampire who'd made his ill intentions clear. He hadn't suffered through years of longing only to lose Lee now, to a vampire who looked like a toy doll in diapers no less.

"Grant, don't be proud," Lee said, infusing a great deal of exasperation in his voice.

Bound with silver chains to a stump of a tree that he'd be able to turn to splinters if he had his full strength—so Grant assumed he didn't—Lee huffed and wheezed. Pale, wan, his ashy skin emphasized the contours of his face, lending his normally elegant features a ghoulish tint. More than anything, Grant wanted to scoop him up and carry his stubborn ass far away from the mess he'd gotten himself into.

Grant said, "I *love* you. Any danger you get into, we're into together. So, maybe hold your temper next time."

"How sweet!" Reggie sneered. "How lucky our precious Lee is!"

Lee narrowed his eyes at Grant's remark, but the flush staining the sharp edges of his cheeks betrayed at least some guilt, possibly shame, for losing control. Later, assuming they made it out alive, Grant would hold Lee's feet to the flames a bit longer. For now, the sheepish expression on Lee's face proved he at least understood how foolhardy he'd been.

"No one wants this to turn deadly. "Be reasonable, be smart," Marcus said, keeping his gaze focused on Reggie. In the same instant, he walked in front of Grant, shielding him from any direct blow.

"But I *am* being reasonable. I want Lee and *only* Lee. The rest of you can go." Reggie concluded his speech by waving them off. The imperious gesture belied how ridiculously harmless he appeared with his curly hair and round, youthful face and slim, petite body.

"You know we can't do that. You're a murderer, Reggie," Marcus said. "We've got to take you to court."

Reggie snorted at Marcus. To the rest of them, he lifted his upper lip to show off his long, yellow-tinged fangs and tilted his chin slightly as though he were about to spit venom. Unsure of the vampire's actual abilities, Grant took a precautionary step backward, at the same time studying his environment in case he needed to dart around to evade an attack. He couldn't float or fly like the vampires, and it wouldn't help anyone if he tripped over vines or stumps.

Reggie shot Grant a contemptuous lip curl. To Marcus, he said, "I can't believe you brought a *dog* to your team. When my maker rode with your crew, they had higher standards."

Marcus didn't acknowledge that Reggie said anything at all. Without warning, he dove for the other vampire, flying at him with electric speed that appeared as little more than blurred lines in Grant's vision. Thrown off his game by the sudden attack, Reggie paused a fraction too long, allowing Marcus to tackle him by wrapping his arms around his knees. The two toppled to the ground in an undignified heap with Marcus's face planted in Reggie's crotch.

The two vampires, scrambling for the upper hand, rolled on the ground, dusting their fancy ball attire in white powdery snow that melted seconds later. Their already dark clothes turned a saturated black. Wet and matted against his forehead, Reggie's curly hair became even more comically cupid, but rage morphed his charming features into a feral mask as he snarled and hissed in fury.

Grant used the opportunity created by the fight to rush to Lee's side. He knelt beside him and ran an exploratory hand over his brow. Lee attempted one of his trademark reassuring smiles but his mouth trembled. "You came to rescue me," he whispered. "I never thought I'd be the boy in the tower."

"Of course I came for you. And it's okay not to be the strong one all the time," Grant said, wiping away a stray tear from Lee's cheek. "Are you hurt?"

Lee shook his head. "Not yet."

"Thank goodness. Let me see what I can do about these chains."

"They're silver. Be careful," Lee reminded him.

Werewolves, like vampires, suffered exhaustion when they interacted with anything silver, so Grant took care not to handle the chains needlessly. He poked and prodded the links around Lee's neck where a single, simple lock kept them connected. Reggie had been too rushed to secure his prisoner properly. A happy accident.

"Hold still," Grant said. "I think I can break the lock."

Hissing through his teeth, Lee lifted his chin to give Grant better access. Beneath the chains, his normally flawless skin had turned a curdled red; deep divots gouged the flesh where the links rested. The sight of the grisly injuries—which would heal in time, Grant comforted himself—spiked Grant's blood pressure. He took a moment to glance over his shoulder, hoping to see Marcus with his boot crushing Reggie's dumb face into the snow. Not quite. But Marcus was at least on top, trying to pin Reggie's flailing arms behind his back.

"Give up!" Marcus shouted at Reggie. The other members of the Silent Crew drew their guns, keeping them aimed at the two combatants while they waited. Neither of them said a word or moved, but their level of professionalism was evident by the steady, never trembling, horizontal hold on their weapons and their unblinking, acute gazes.

"Get off me!" Reggie shouted. He reared his arm all the way back, then launched his fist into Marcus's face. "Off, off, off."

Marcus flinched at each blow but tightened his grip on the vampire's other wrist. Gritting his teeth with the effort, he held fast as Reggie bucked with all the strength and madness at his disposal. To Grant's dismay, Reggie proved more powerful than the stalwart Marcus. Screaming a ferocious battle cry, the smaller vampire hurled his opponent directly at the other two members of the Silent Crew and whirled to face Grant.

"Hurry," Lee said. "Snap off these chains."

Being as careful as possible to avoid Lee's injuries, Grant pawed at the ridiculously small lock, fumbling with his large sausage-like fingers.

"Don't be coy with the thing. You're not on a date with it!" Lee chastised him.

"Yes, yes, yes."

Grant clutched the two ends. Using all his strength and ignoring the agony of the silver searing his skin, he yanked the chain apart. The frail metal lock snapped just as Reggie crashed into his side, the force of the blow propelling him against the tree. Dazed, tasting the copper of blood, Grant tried to shake off the effects of the blow and rise from the ground, but the jabbing pain shooting from his side made a minor amount of movement almost unbearable.

"You should have stayed where I put you," Reggie sneered. "Now you're going to die right alongside Lee. How romantic, right?"

Reggie, arm raised above his head as he readied the killing blow, stalked forward. His yellow eyes, red-tinged in the pupils, narrowed on Grant's face; then, suddenly, they opened as wide as quarters and his jaw dropped. Half conscious and fading fast, Grant lunged right as Lee wrapped a silver chain around Reggie's throat. Snarling, he dragged the enraged vampire backward and then tossed him at Marcus's feet.

Weakened by the silver, Reggie hissed, cussed, and raged, but he remained where he was—defeated at last and cuffed moments later.

Marcus grinned. "Nicely done, you two. You're quite the team."

Lee spared Marcus a quick "Thank you." Dropping down beside Grant, a worried frown creasing his brow, he asked, "Are you going to heal all right?"

Grant gave his cheek a fond pat. "Only if you insist."

Grinning big, Lee nuzzled his nose against Grant's. "I command it. And then carry me home the same way you carried that carriage-driving chump."

Chapter Forty-Four

Behind Grant, Lee hummed a happy tune as he packed the rest of his belongings. As was typical, he tossed his clothing into a big heap, and then used his vampire strength to squish everything down and zip the suitcase shut. That pretty much settled who'd do the laundry in their life of marital bliss to come. Grant would also think twice before accepting a hand job after Lee furiously pumped the handle of the suitcase into its casing, outright jamming it when it refused to go gently.

"What are you smirking about?" Lee asked.

"You doing the monster mash with your belongings. Remind me never to leave my delicates in your hands. What about you? What's got your lips twitching?"

Obviously trying to keep his smirk from spreading to a full-blown high-beam grin, Lee said, "Oh, dear heart, I'm happy because your declaration of love didn't involve disaster cupcakes and a moonlight chase. Got off pretty easy."

"Never too late for a hunt." Grant raised his hands above his head and curled his fingers into claws. Walking on his tiptoes, his incisors dangling, Grant stalked over toward Lee, stopping to wrap him in a massive hug that his friend, a lover at last, endured with little grumbling.

"Okay, let me go. Tokyo is that way, Godzilla," Lee grumbled without fang.

Grant snorted into the back of Lee's head but loosened his hold. They stayed rooted to the spot, swaying in time to the rhythm between them; Grant closed his eyes to fully enjoy the moment, the first of many to come across a sea of years.

"You packed already?" Lee asked. He covered Grant's hand with his own and squeezed.

"Um-hum. An hour ago. And my bags are already in the car."

"Okay, let's get out of here."

Grant carried down Lee's bags while Lee covered the last-minute scan of the room. Not that it mattered. He *always* left something behind. This time, Grant hoped he broke the trend. He didn't want to drive three hundred miles to get a toothbrush Lee couldn't live without. Grant would do it—because love—but he'd expect an amazing blowjob for the effort. On second thought, Lee forgetting something didn't sound so bad.

A familiar scent stopped Grant in his tracks. He stuck his nose in the air to confirm the impossible. Yup. Lucky—the missing rabbit. "Son of a gun," Grant said, a wide grin spreading across his face.

Shadows so dense they blotted out the glimmering white of the snow partially obscured the forest floor. Even with his enhanced vision, Grant had to squint to pierce the pitch-black veil. As he approached, an animal scurried in the brush. Grant hadn't seen Lucky yet but the telltale snapping of small branches and the faint crunch of snow, not to mention the stench, told him what his eyes couldn't—the rabbit was there.

Grant knelt to get a better view of the forest floor. The loose rocks of the drive dug into his knees, no doubt leaving pebble-shaped indents in his flesh. The small jabs of pain were worth it. Right in front of him, behind a small patch of wild rose, the long ear of his favorite rabbit trembled in the wind.

Hey, buddy. No need to bolt. I'm a friendly werewolf.

Keeping low, barely trusting himself to move, Grant inched forward by using his hands to maintain balance. Up ahead, Lucky hopped in a small circle; his nose and ears twitching as he searched for what precious little food the forest offered in the dead of winter.

If Lucky could be persuaded, Grant might have suggested a mutually beneficial relationship where Grant would provide plenty of food if Lucky vowed to snuggle Lee until he was as blissfully happy as a fuzzy rodent could make him. *A cute fuzzy rodent*, Grant admitted to himself, something he'd never confess out loud.

Grant crept toward Lucky, stopping whenever the rabbit seemed wise to his presence or when the damn thing appeared about to bolt for some other reason. Small animals were skittish, and Grant only had one shot; he couldn't very well rip off his clothes and chase Lucky down as a wolf. The hotel management made it quite clear they were to be gone by ten, and they were pushing that deadline as it was.

Okay, here goes nothing.

Grant lunged forward, using all his forward momentum to clear the distance between him and Lucky. As he flew through the air, it occurred to him that Lee transformed him into the most ridiculous werewolf ever to live, a seven-foot predator who'd evolved to hunting down pet bunnies, and he loved him all the more for it.

The air evacuated Grant's lungs in a burning *whoosh* as his chest thumped against the hard ground. Lucky wiggled in his hands and belted out his characteristic death cry. Grant clutched him to his chest while the poor thing cried out and twisted frantically. The rabbit's heart beat wildly in a pattern that Grant's highly evolved brain understood—total fear. Catching him as a grand romantic gesture toward Lee seemed good on paper, but Grant was beginning to feel like an ass.

Grant stood and drew the rabbit against his chest. Keeping his voice low, as soothing as he could manage with such a deep baritone, Grant said, "You're okay, buddy. I promise I won't hurt you."

Lucky didn't seem convinced, but at least he didn't shriek in response.

Grant smiled, sans sharp teeth. "Hey, you can sense that I'd eat you if left to my own devices, but I'm in love, and my partner would eat me if I chomped you down."

The rabbit's ear twitched.

"That's right. Big bad wolf can't use his teeth. I've got corks on my fangs."

Lucky flopped in his arms, stretching out from wrist to elbow. Befuddled by the sudden turnaround, not quite trusting it, Grant risked a slight head pat between Lucky's silky ears, just to see if the tricky critter was trying to pull one over on him. The rabbit's heartbeat remained steady, and his eyes had lost the manic gleam. In fact, he rolled right over in Grant's arms. Grant huffed at the sudden, complete reversal.

"What's up, Doc?" Grant whispered, giving the docile bunny's head a sniff, just to make sure it wasn't some type of demon trying to lull him into a false sense of security. "Do you believe me that rabbit season is over?"

Comfortable enough to be curious, Lucky sniffed Grant's fingers, nibbling a tiny bit at the tips of his fingernails. Not used to handling anything so fragile,

Grant struggled to master his grip. Holding too tightly might squish Lucky. Facing Lee splattered with bunnywuv guts...obviously bad. But he didn't want to loosen his grip and accidently drop the rabbit either. Grant tried to split the difference and bounced Lucky from one hand to the other, kind of like a slinky.

From above him—far, far above—Lee chuckled.

"Lee! You glamor this rabbit again?" Grant shouted, happy and annoyed simultaneously. "Seriously?"

Holding his hands triumphantly above his head, Lee floated toward Grant. As he landed, his grin, more mischievous than the Cheshire cat's, spread to an impossible length until Lee was all dimples, teeth, and fabulous good humor. He held out his hands for the rabbit, curling his fingers and repeating "Gimmie" when Grant held back.

"Okay, here's your bunnywuvs," Grant said.

Lee nabbed the bunny and lifted him to eye level. Lucky's nose twitched, his eyes dilated, and for a moment, he looked like he was about ready to shoot out an arsenal of butt pellets. Lee said, "*Blah*, you will never be afraid of Grant again. *Blah*!" To Grant, he said, "Ta-da! He'll love werewolves now forever and ever!"

"Wow? Really?"

Lee snickered. "*No*, dear heart. As soon as the glamour wears off, Lucky is going to hop for his life to the nearest phone and call Van Helsing."

"He takes house calls from rabbits, does he?"

"Sure, why not? Also, I've enjoyed watching you hold Lucky with your big, strong, tender hands. You want to keep at it? I'll wait."

"Yeah," Grant admitted. "I really do."

Lee leaned against Grant's back while he enjoyed the novelty of a creature as small and skittish as a rabbit lounging against him as though he were little more than a poolside lounge chair. And, you know, not a giant man who transformed into a gargantuan wolf—sharp teeth, claws, and a constantly rumbling tummy that sounded an awful lot like a deep growl. Grant tried not to succumb to the fit of sentimentality threatening to change him into something far more dangerous than a beast—a sap.

Lee sniffled and did that thing he did whenever he wanted something but didn't quite know how to ask: a little shuffle dance Grant liked to call the cha-cha-make-me-a-chump because Grant *always* caved.

"Spit it out. I can sense your thoughts churning over there."

Without further preamble, Lee blurted, "*Blah*, I vant to adopt some kids with you. *Blah.*"

On reflex, Grant dropped Lucky. After one pointed annoyed look over his shoulder as if to say *Good luck with the whole kid thing*, the rabbit scampered away, never to be seen again. Three years later, Grant would think fondly back on this moment as he cradled Leveret, his and Lee's first adopted child, against his shoulder. Their hearts beat steadily, eerily synchronized, while they shared a chuckle at Grant's bubbly baby talk.

Right now, in this moment with Lee waiting to hear a response, Grant's heart practically pried open the bars of his ribcage and absconded, waving attached arteries over its head like flailing arms. Behind it, trailed a legion of children with goobered fingers and poop butt. Hearts can't smell, of course, but it knew enough to be worried.

"Well?" Lee prodded. "What do you think?"

"That's a huge step."

"I *know*. Do you want to walk in that direction too?"

Just as suddenly as it came, the dire vision of grungy children trailing after Grant, while he tried his best to escape unscathed, vanished. In its place, he envisioned himself and Lee teaching baby Leveret to gently pet the longhaired cat they'd be sure to adopt as a family. Leveret—his eyes blue, green, no, brown—would flicker in delight when the kitten purred and bopped its head against his. They'd have family bikes, a garden filled with radishes, tomatoes, and cucumbers, and a whole mess of scrapbooks that got less sloppy as their son aged.

"Yes, yes. I *do* want that."

And so he let go of trying to get lucky and grabbed hold of Lee's hand.

Acknowledgements

Thank you to my family and friends for their continued support. Also, as always, I want to thank NineStar Press for giving my books a home and BJ for making sure eyeballs aren't rolling around the room in my manuscripts.

About the Author

Jacqueline Rohrbach is a 36-year-old creative writer living in windy central Washington. When she isn't writing strange books about bloodsucking magical werewolves, she's baking sweets, or walking her two dogs, Nibbler and Mulder. She also loves cheesy ghost shows, especially when the hosts call out the ghost out like he wants to brawl with it in a bar. You know, "Come out here, you coward! You like to haunt little kids. Haunt me!" Jackee laughs at this EVERY time.

She's also a hopeless World of Warcraft addict. In her heyday, she was a top parsing disc priest. She became a paladin to fight Deathwing, she went back to a priest to cuddle pandas, and then she went to a shaman because I guess she thought it would be fun to spend an entire expansion underpowered and frustrated. Boomchicken for Legion!

Email: Jackeeroh@gmail.com

Twitter: @JackeeRohrbach

Website: www.jackeewrites.com

Other NineStar books by this author

The Worst Werewolf
The False Moon
Just in Time
Speak with the Dead
Parallel Larry
The Dragon's Rebel
The Soulstealers

Also Available from NineStar Press

Connect with NineStar Press

www.ninestarpress.com

www.facebook.com/ninestarpress

www.facebook.com/groups/NineStarNiche

www.twitter.com/ninestarpress